Home to Roost

HOME TO ROOST

Gerald Hammond

St. Martin's Press
New York

Library of Congress Cataloging-in-Publication Data

Hammond, Gerald
  Home to roost / Gerald Hammond.
     p.   cm.
  ISBN 0-312-06369-5
  I. Title.
  PR6058.A55456H66   1991
  823'.914—dc20   91-20061
                                                         CIP

First published in Great Britain by Macmillan London Limited.

First U.S. Edition: December 1991
10 9 8 7 6 5 4 3 2 1

Home to Roost

ONE

The Pentland Gun Club was usually quiet on week-day afternoons. The end of the game and wildfowling seasons had brought out a few fanatics, but a sky the colour of the local stone and a wind coming down the valley straight from the North Pole had sent some of them home in short time. We were paying dearly for a fine summer which had followed a winter so mild that gardeners had complained of having to mow grass. But summer had ended in the wettest autumn on record and since then the rain had alternated with frost and gales and occasional snow.

When a sudden shower of sleet put an end to the afternoon's activity, I would have been relieved at being driven back into the warm clubhouse, except that I was on form while Deborah, who suffers from cold fingers but hates to shoot in gloves, was not. We had been neck and neck on the Sporting layout with only my favourite Springing Teal to come when the sleet, and the squally wind on which it arrived, had driven us indoors.

Sometimes it seems inevitable that Deborah and I will marry. At other times that seems, if not impossible, at least a recipe for disaster.

Our relationship must fall somewhere within the many definitions of love. Yet twice we have turned back from the very brink of becoming engaged. Once, she balked at the idea of attaching herself permanently to a detective sergeant – not, I honestly believe, because of any uncertainty about pay or prospects but because her background had taught her only too well the risks to which a police officer, who must expect at least once in his service to face up to an armed criminal, is exposing himself.

On the other occasion, it was I who got cold feet. Deborah is a delightful person to have around. As a girl, she is a magnet for male eyes. Even when she is dressed for ratting or ferreting – as I first saw her – there is no doubt of her gamine charm, but when she takes trouble over her appearance she is, in a youthful way, much more than pretty. There is a hint of beauty to follow on when she loses the last traces of puppy-fat. (They say that you should look at the mother, and Molly Calder is a lovely woman.) Deborah's figure is all girl, the soft roundness belying the well-developed musculature beneath. At times there is twined around us a net of mutual desire – we know it and others can see it. And yet it is not desire that draws us together but simple pleasure in each other's company. And a shared sense of humour. We can reduce each other to tears of laughter over some ridiculous piece of imagery.

Looking back over what I have written, it reads like the specification for a long and happy marriage. So why did I hesitate? I asked myself the same question and did not like the answer, which was quite simply masculine pride. The uncomfortable fact was that marriage to Deborah would entail a high risk of role reversal. Not that I would be left at home in a frilly apron, minding the baby and collecting recipes. I may be a better cook than Deborah, but she has a well-developed nesting instinct. Her earning capability, although good, is sporadic. On the other hand if Keith, her father, should ever decide to retire – a contingency which looks at the moment to be remote in the extreme – she is more than competent to inherit his half of the family business. For the moment, she is content to divide her time between helping her father in the shop and at the workbench, and sharing the running of the Pentland Gun Club with a retired schoolmaster who looks after the daily management while she organises the competitions and undertakes the coaching.

Problems are for solving, and I dare say that I could have come to terms with having a wife who would one day bring money into the family. Deborah has a strong personality, but I could accept a marriage which was a partnership rather than a relationship between master and slave.

The real barrier, I am ashamed to say, is deeper and yet more trivial. We had hardly met before Deborah infected me with her own passion for the sport of clay pigeon shooting. Unfortunately, she is very good at it. According to Keith, a young girl with good reflexes, properly taught, can become devastatingly good, and Deborah is the living, breathing, shooting proof of it. She had been shooting since she was first old enough to swing a cut-down four-ten and Keith is a first-class coach. She rarely enters a ladies' match at Skeet or Sporting without lifting a prize or a trophy; and even among men in open competition she is usually fighting it out with the leaders. Some of them resent it and, against my own better instincts, I am one of them. I could be proud of a wife who bested me in art or at chess; but shooting is a male preserve, bound up with the male prerogative of gathering meat, and my ego rebels at the idea of a wife who can shoot better than I can.

I said as much to Deborah once, just before we

went out for a round of Skeet. I said it lightly, hoping that she would take it as a joke, but she probably saw through me. She shot a clean round, twenty-five straight, besting me by four, and said that she supposed that she would just have to die an old maid.

'That's the risk you're taking,' I said.

She hid her teeth behind her lips. 'You rang, my lord?' she asked in a quavering voice. A few seconds later, we were giggling together over a vision of her as an ageing version of the maid in a French farce. The moment had passed by but my pique had not.

Some day, I promised myself, I would beat her, just once. Then and only then would I let her sweep me off my feet.

There were only four of us, a small group in the big room. Deborah had been booked for a coaching session on the high tower. Her pupil, a sturdy man in tweed trousers and a well-worn Goretex coat and hat, joined us at the bar and offered us a drink. He laid a good quality over-under across one of the tables. Without the hat I saw that he had wiry grey hair above a round, red face.

Sam Pollinder, the retired schoolteacher who shared the running of the club, was tending the bar between fussing with some papers. He was a mediocre shot – after only a few months of practice and with the benefit of Deborah's tuition I could nearly always improve on his scores – but an asset to the club. Round, balding and squeaky, he came over as a fusspot; but he was a heaven-sent administrator. Anything that he took on, including the Pentland Gun Club, ran on the proverbial oiled wheels.

'I doubt there'll be any more shooting today,' he said. 'Non-drivers can have a proper drink.' Until shooting was over, the club served – and permitted – only low-alcohol drinks.

10

'I'd be on my own,' I said. Deborah had brought me in her father's jeep. But beyond the broad windows I could see only the jeep and the ex-teacher's red hatchback.

'My wife dropped me off,' the other man said. 'She went on to the Country Club for a sauna. She's making one last-ditch attempt to get her weight down below mine. She'll pick me up later. Her sister's looking after the . . . the place,' he explained unnecessarily. 'You'll take a dram, lad?'

I accepted a dram, which turned out to be a large Glenfiddich, and made a mental note to avoid his company in future whenever the usual restriction was lifted. He could prove to be expensive company. Sam Pollinder accepted his usual alcohol-free lager and Deborah the same, diluted even further into a shandy.

'Are you turning out again on Saturday?' Sam asked Deborah.

She shrugged. 'Are you on duty, that day, Ian?' she asked me.

'Not if the citizenry behaves itself,' I said.

'The club will be closed anyway. It's the second and final day of the Borders Pigeon-Shoot. Your chance to try yourself out against the real thing, if you want to. Don't expect too much, though. We drew a stretch of low-ground forestry which hardly attracted a single bird. We could see them dropping into the beech-woods half a mile away.'

I gave the question some thought. I had been conditioned by my upbringing and by my police background to believe that all gun-owners were irresponsible sadists if not actively criminal. My involvement with the clay-shooting fraternity had driven a wedge into that belief. There had remained a gut feeling that to kill a living creature had to be wrong, although when challenged by

11

Deborah I was unable to explain why that should be so if it was acceptable to eat meat killed by somebody else. Several days spent in her company, beating at various shoots, had shown me some of the magic of a winter's day spent in the pursuit of pheasant or partridge and the artistry which went into presenting the birds as suitably challenging targets; and I had found that the participants were individuals not greatly different from myself. They were prepared to work for their sport and they respected their quarry. But while I began to appreciate their way of life I had so far not lifted a gun against a live target.

While I thought it over, Sam was speaking again, rather defensively. 'It was the luck of the draw,' he said. 'And that area can be good, some years. You'd have been all right if the beech-woods had been better covered.'

'But they weren't,' Deborah pointed out. 'The gutless wonders you put there went home before roosting time. It was too cold for them. Can you promise me that it won't happen again?'

'No,' Sam said frankly. 'But I can do better than that. I can move you. How would Nuttleigh's Farm suit you?'

She lit up as another girl might have done at the sight of a diamond ring. 'Great!' she said. 'I passed there yesterday and the barley's still drawing them. But the shooting there belongs to the McKimber Estate. I think it's let to Jeffries, the game farm man. Don't tell me that they've given up the shooting rights? Because Dad would—'

'Nothing like that. But some of the men who drew McKimber last week have gone off for a winter break and I'm having to move people around. I have to keep the best woods covered or the birds will go plop in there and the Guns round about will do their nuts.'

12

'Hey!' said the other man. 'If there's room for a little one, I'll have some of that.'

'You, Mr Kerr?' Sam said. 'I thought you had a farm of your own thereabouts.'

'Next door,' Mr Kerr said. 'But I've no roosting wood on it. It'll be twenty years before the trees I've planted are used as a roost. I've had some sport with the cushies, but the stubbles are ploughed now and the rape's betwixt and between.'

Dark clouds had blotted out the daylight. Sam got up and switched on the lights. The big room, which had looked funereal, cheered up immediately.

Deborah, who would have been hard put to it to name her Member of Parliament, had an encyclopaedic knowledge of the local farms. 'Who farms Nuttleigh's these days?' she asked.

'Nuttleigh, I presume,' I said.

She looked at me in scorn. 'The last Nuttleigh died around the time of Bannockburn,' she said. 'Brian Dunbar, isn't it? You used to be as thick as thieves with him,' she told Mr Kerr. 'Surely you can shoot there any time.'

Mr Kerr looked out of the window. The sleet had turned to rain. 'The way things are,' he said, 'I'd rather not ask for favours.'

It seemed to be time to turn the subject. 'I've got nothing against pigeon,' I said. 'They've never done me any harm.'

The others flinched. Evidently I had uttered a heresy. 'A woodpigeon can fill its crop with about four ounces of grain, more than once a day,' Deborah said. 'The last estimate I saw reckoned that there were about ten million in the country. They can raise two or three broods a year, two squabs at a time. It takes about a pound and a half of grain to make a loaf. Work it out for yourself.'

13

'And that's not counting incidental damage,' Mr Kerr said gloomily. 'Like the seed they knock down when they're feeding on rape before harvest time. Far more than they eat.'

I bought him a drink to cheer him up and told Deborah that, all right, I'd try myself out on real pigeon. If I didn't like it, I could always go home.

'What'll we be doing?' I asked.

'Roost shooting,' she said. 'Pigeon aren't easy to control. You can decoy them. Sometimes it works and sometimes it doesn't. Or, if you're lucky, you can get under a flight-line. Or you can shoot them when they come in to roost. The only way to make a real dent in their numbers is to have all favourite roosting places covered at the same time. When it's beginning to get dark, they make up their little minds that they're going to come in somewhere. If they're shot at in one place, they move on to another.'

'It sounds too easy,' I said.

'We'll see if you're still saying that on Saturday night,' she retorted.

When I first met Deborah, I was a detective sergeant with the Lothian and Borders Constabulary, stationed in Edinburgh. With her help, I arrived at the solution to a murder case in advance of my superiors. Or, to be more honest, she arrived at it with minimal assistance from me, although she insisted that I take the credit.

A month or so later, I was posted to Newton Lauder. This, I suspect, was not a reward for my zeal but a banishment to the local equivalent of Siberia. Superiors in general, and Superintendent McHarg in particular, do not appreciate being beaten to the punch by junior officers – or 'having their eyes wiped' in the language

14

of the dog world which I was rapidly learning from Deborah and her family.

The posting pleased me until the snags began to surface. Newton Lauder is a charming old town in the Scottish Borders. Deborah lived with her parents in Briesland House, a mile or two outside the town, so that my relationship with her – call it an affair, a courting or just friendship, whatever you will – no longer suffered the impediment of distance. And I was a long way from Superintendent McHarg.

Although Newton Lauder was the headquarters for the policing of a large area, it was not a hotbed of crime. The CID was represented there by a sergeant and a constable, the rare crime of any seriousness being handled from Edinburgh. I was now that sergeant and the constable's post was vacant. Which suited me very well. Newton Lauder might experience the occasional murder or serious assault, but the general run of crime was represented by petty pilfering or an outbreak of graffiti on the walls of the secondary school.

The snag was that I had to serve two masters – and, worse, two masters who disliked each other intensely – and each used me as a stick with which to prod the other. To McHarg, in Edinburgh, I was responsible whenever a crime occurred, but I looked to the local Chief Superintendent, a Hebridean teetering on the edge of retirement, for matters of administration; and by long-standing agreement Chief Superintendent Munro was to make use of my time whenever no local crimes required my attention.

Over many years Mr Munro and Deborah's father had overcome the mistrust inevitable between a conservative policeman and a dealer in guns, and had arrived at a state of truce bordering on real friendship. Never one to miss a chance, Mr Munro had decided to capitalise on my friendship with the Calder family and, taking advantage of his local responsibility for crime prevention (as opposed to detection), had appointed me as his Firearms Officer to oversee an otherwise civilian staff; thereby, at a single stroke, infuriating Mr McHarg, obtaining expert advice free of charge and going some way towards meeting his obligations under the new firearms legislation.

It was this duty that took me out to the McKimber Estate on the day after our visit to the Gun Club. Nothing in the new Act required such a visit to inspect the storage of shotguns, although some chief officers were stretching their powers with the intention of discouraging the private ownership of guns; but the head keeper at McKimber had made one of the first applications on the new form and had been as confused as everybody else as to how to present a clear listing of his guns. A visit seemed to be called for.

My predecessor (as Firearms Officer) had left a map pinned to the wall of what was now my office. Many of the boundaries of farms and estates were marked on the map. I glanced at it to make sure of my route. The McKimber Estate, I noticed, included several thousand acres of mixed woodland, giving way gradually to farmland on the boundary. Miscally, Ian Kerr's farm, caught my eye, lying just outside the boundary.

Frost had returned overnight. I used an aerosol to clear a patch through the fern-pictures on the windscreen and left it to the heater to do the rest. Once off the main road, ice lay wherever the tarmac was shaded but the gravel road to the big house offered a better grip. A woman in an apron answered the doorbell. She made it clear that policemen were expected to come to the back door, that the keeping staff had nothing to do with the household and in any case were far below the

16

dignity of her attention, but she managed to direct me to the head keeper's cottage which was tucked out of sight beyond gardens which, even in the dead of winter, could be seen to be in need of regular professional attention. The keeper's house turned out to be a small villa, probably once a dower house, and in considerably better taste than its larger neighbour although the lay-out was marred by a rambling assembly of kennels and sheds.

Mrs Brindle, the head keeper's wife, was younger than I expected, a fluffy blonde with a chubby body and come-hither eyes. I identified myself and explained my errand.

'He's away out around the pens,' she said, 'catching up birds for next season's rearing. You could find him. But if it would save fetching him back, would you like to see his guns?'

I followed her into the house. She fiddled with a combination padlock to open the door of a small room where the guns were racked. The window was stoutly barred.

Most of my questions answered themselves, but there were several points to be checked. Mrs Brindle, who had been lurking at my elbow – whether to prevent me tampering with the guns or for the sake of male companionship I had no way of knowing – shied away when I asked her a question.

'I'd better see him,' I said.

'There's only the one estate road makes a ring around the place,' she said. 'There are side-tracks, but you can see along them. Watch for a grey, long-chassis Land-Rover.'

I bumped halfway around the frozen mud of the estate road. The woods were not the usual coniferous plantations, put in for the grants and then forgotten, but a mixture of deciduous forest trees and low conifers, split into wandering fingers of woodland around glades and clearings and broad rides. They would be beautiful in summer, but I decided that they had been planned for the shooting rather than for amenity value.

I spotted the grey Land-Rover a hundred yards up a ride which led through a beech-wood towards a glow of open sky beyond. In a small pen containing a blue-painted pheasant feeder and a drinker, a man in a stiff tweed suit and gaiters, assisted by a youth in his late teens, was catching pheasants, examining each one critically before either releasing it outside the pen or stuffing it into a large, plastic crate. An old but well-kept side-by-side shotgun lay against the wire. A sleek black Labrador lay motionless beside the pen, watching me with suspicious eyes.

The older of the two men looked at me with similar mistrust. He was in his thirties, strong-featured with a mop of black, curly hair only partially concealed by a fore-and-aft hat which matched the tweed of his suit. (The youth, I noticed, was wearing breeks of the same tweed which I guessed to be the estate uniform.)

'What are you doing here?' he asked abruptly.

Keepers are rightly suspicious of anyone wandering on their territory. I took the question at face value, introduced myself and explained my errand.

Mr Brindle was not mollified. 'More bloody bureaucracy!' he complained. 'There was no need for you to come out here. I ken fine what you're up to. Running up the costs of the new legislation to justify an increase in the fees, pricing gun-ownership out of the reach of the working man! If you'd do something about the bloody poachers you'd do more to earn your keep.' He tossed a gaudy cock pheasant outside. It gobbled indignantly but strolled off, unperturbed. 'That beggar's in here every

18

day, helping himself to feed instead of having to scratch for it in a strawed ride. He kens damned fine he's safe now.' Brindle smiled grimly. 'If he hopes I'll take him along to the hens, he's got another think coming. I've more than enough cocks.'

'If you have a problem with poachers,' I said, 'it's the first I've heard of it. Let's talk about it.'

He looked at me hard, seeing me for the first time as a person rather than as an annoying figure of authority. 'What do you want?' he asked more mildly.

'Your application for a renewal of your shotgun certificate,' I said. 'There were some unclear points. It seemed easier for both of us if I came out for a chat instead of trying to deal by phone or letter.'

He nodded. 'You carry on,' he said to his young assistant. 'I'll be watching. Now, what are these points?'

I looked down at my notes. 'I've cleared most of them up,' I said. 'Your wife showed me the guns—'

'*She did what?* You'd no business. The new law gives you no power to inspect.'

So he was a barrack-room lawyer. I chose my words carefully. 'The Firearms Act gives me the right, and you have rifles in the same room. Anyway, your wife invited me inside. I didn't ask her.'

'If you're going to be technical . . .'

'If I was going to be technical,' I said, 'I could point out that your wife had access to the guns and, not holding a certificate, she's an unauthorised person. Under the Nineteen Sixty-eight Act, Section Fifty-two, I could confiscate your guns.' He changed colour and gaped at me. 'But I'm not unreasonable and I'm not going to be technical.'

'But you were having a snoop at my security.'

'I wasn't. But I could hardly help noticing.' I paused and he glared at me. 'I noticed the oak door, the

19

security lock and the bars on the window. I also noticed the dog's basket just outside the door. As long as the house is occupied, I'll accept that. Of course, if you leave it empty—'

'We're not ones for holidays,' he said, 'even if a keeper could spare the time or the money. If we go away it's for a night or two and one of my under-keepers sleeps in.'

'That's all right, then,' I said. I nodded at the shotgun. 'I take it that that's the McNaughton gun that was absent from your rack?'

He nodded.

'You've applied for certificates for your two under-keepers but no guns are specified. They'll use guns out of your gunroom?'

'When they need them.'

'Fine, as long as they're kept securely overnight.'

We tidied up a couple of minor, technical questions. 'That's all that I needed,' I said. 'Do you want to tell me about your poachers?'

He drew a deep breath and let it out again. 'I thought you were going to ask for security cabinets and electronic alarms,' he said more mildly. 'And I don't see my boss paying good money for such-like, not here. He'll have all the latest at his own home, no doubt of it.'

He stopped and, while he thought, he pulled out an old pipe and a pouch. When his pipe was drawing nicely he said through the smoke, 'This time of year, we're still catching up pheasants, hens mostly, for egg-laying.'

'And release them again as soon as they've raised their chicks?'

He shook his head. Evidently I had exposed my ignorance. 'Sooner than that. Soon as they've finished laying,' he said, 'they're out. Pheasants don't make

20

good mothers. The eggs go into electric incubators and the chicks into brooders. We've been poached, off and on, all winter, but while we're catching up we're specially vulnerable. We've four catching pens – d'you see? – and we can't watch 'em all. Not the whole time. Some slippery sod who kens the ground well keeps helping himself.'

I nodded sympathetically. From Deborah and her father I had learned something of the economics of poaching. This was a commercial shoot, where businessmen coming for a day's driven shooting paid perhaps twice what each bird had cost to rear. The game dealer would pay the shoot operator or the poacher only a fraction of the rearing cost. The poacher was therefore removing from the ground an asset of considerably greater value than he would be paid for it. Whatever one's views might be of that type of sport, the keeper, whose livelihood might depend on showing a good return, had every right to feel aggrieved at what was, after all was said and done, robbery – and often armed robbery.

'Why haven't I heard about this before?' I asked him.

He shrugged and turned away, picking up a thumb-stick which lay beside his gun. Evidently I was expected to walk with him. The dog lay still until a flick of a finger called him tight to his master's heel. It was good to move again, walking over the crunching leaves. The sun had come out and frost was melting and dripping from the branches overhead.

'I reported the first occurrences to Newton Lauder,' Brindle said. 'Seems they still think of the poacher as a poor, starving old peasant feeding his family on nature's bounty which the wicked laird wants to keep for hisself. They equip themselves with the latest technology but

21

their thinking's a hundred years out of date. I gave up after a bittie. You'll do the same. They'll not want you to take an interest.'

'You're wrong,' I told him. 'Especially about the latest technology. I come under Edinburgh, not Newton Lauder. If I report the matter to my chiefs in Edinburgh, I think they'll let me follow it up. What can you tell me about your poacher?'

He stopped and leaned on his stick. We had come to where the trees stopped at a hedge and the ground fell away steeply to a fence at the bottom. Below us, open Borders farmland was spread in a winter patchwork of plough and grass and stubble. I started picking out landmarks. Below me a digging machine – a JCB, I thought – was noisily cutting a scar across the countryside, through a field where some cereal crop had been left unharvested. Ahead of it, to my left, a line of large pipes laid on the ground marched away into the distance.

'What's happening down there?' I asked.

'Water main.'

'What about your poacher?'

'He kens the ground as well as I do myself,' Brindle said. 'During the winter, he was using a lamp and an air rifle, knocking the pheasants out of their roosts. He was coming about once a week, on average, but not regular. We kept watch and spotted the light of his lamp more'n once but we could never come up wi' him. He has a dog wi'm to give warning – a wee dog, from the tracks, no' a big bogger like Seamus here. This time of year he finds it easier to raid the catching pens – and any birds that he leaves behind are too unsettled to mate for a fortnight,' Brindle added bitterly. 'I'd be feared that he was at one of the other catchers this minute, except that he's seldom here midweek in daylight. I jalouse that he has a daytime job or a business of his own.

'And he has a freezer, or access to a cold store. A game dealer wouldn't be buying pheasants just now, not without wanting to know where they came from after the season's finished, so my mannie'll be putting them by to take out at the beginning of next season when the price is above rock-bottom.'

I was making notes – not that my memory was untrustworthy, but notes made at the time can lend support to evidence given later. 'Anything else?' I asked.

'Aye there's more. I've followed his tracks often enough. He wears the common, black welly, size nine. There's been times I've been so close ahint him that I could see where he's brushed the dew off a fir-tree. From that, and the length of his stride, I'd say that he's not more than average height and most likely less. I've found matches but never a tabbie, so he smokes on the job – there's no' many poachers do that – and if it's the ciggies and no' a pipe then he's a damned carefu' man. He comes and goes by a different road each time. Usually he's on his ownsome and takes just as many birds as he can carry in a jute sack – I've seen the imprint of it where he set it down on a patch of mud. But twice there's been another man wi' him.'

Mr Brindle paused, thought deeply and then gave a grunt to signify that he had no more to offer me.

'Can you tell me anything about the other man?' I asked him.

'Smaller boot, a seven. Not so heavy. Could be a woman or a teenager. And it was daytime, both times he – or she – came along.'

I remembered one of Deborah's father's anecdotes about poaching. 'You didn't notice a woman with a pram walking a baby through the estate, either time?'

23

His full lips twisted into a sneer. 'I'm not as green as I'm cabbage-looking,' he said. Evidently he had heard the same story of poached pheasants carried off in a perambulator.

'This damned pigeon-shoot,' he said suddenly. 'It's out of my hands, I'm just told to co-operate and find places for our beaters and whoever yon mannie Pollinder sends me. Every Tom, Dick and Harry with permission to bring their guns on to the estate.' He straightened up and began to ram down his thumbstick to lend emphasis to his words. 'Rag, tag and bobtail, all the scruffs from the beating line, shots going off all around, how the hell am I supposed to know it's all pigeon that's being shot?'

His words reminded me. 'I'm coming to the pigeon-shoot on Saturday. That's Nuttleigh's Farm below us, isn't it?'

'That's right. Damn't, I wish I'd known. I could fine be doing with a policeman among the Guns. But all the corners are spoken for now. So you shoot, do you?'

'Clay pigeons, mostly.' I was damned if I was going to admit that Saturday would be my first attempt at a live target. 'One of your neighbours is joining us on Nuttleigh's on Saturday. Ian Kerr. Which is his farm?'

Mr Brindle nodded to our left, towards what I thought was the north. 'The open ground beyond the trees,' he said shortly, and clamped his mouth shut. It seemed that Mr Kerr was not a favourite with him.

'About your poacher,' I said. I save a few slips of blank paper in the back of my notebook. I wrote my home phone number on one of them and handed it to him. 'If you can't reach me through the police, call me at home. Can you give me a map of the estate? Mark on it a few suitable rendezvous points and give them names or letters. And do you have walkie-talkies?'

He nodded. 'We use them on shoot days. They're idle now.'

'I suggest that you lend me one and carry another. Then if you have to call me out we can keep in touch.'

He nodded again, looking a little less fierce. 'Pick it up, and the map, on your way to Nuttleigh's on Saturday,' he said. 'Now I'd better get back and see what's going wrong. These MSC laddies . . .'

As we walked back towards the vehicles he made conversation about the weather and the prospect for the pigeon-shoot. I felt that I had passed a test and I was oddly gratified.

There was nothing of any urgency to require my attention back at Headquarters. On the other hand, there was a good chance that Deborah would be at home. I drove round the town and turned off to Briesland House.

It was as well that among Brindle's guns I had found a reasonable excuse to visit Keith Calder. When Molly, Deborah's mother, sent me into Keith's study, I found Chief Superintendent Munro taking coffee with Keith, very much at his ease. He sat up and glared at me. Keith, with a glint of mildly malicious amusement in his eye, waved me to a chair and poured coffee into a spare cup.

'Deborah's out,' he said.

'I knew that,' I said, thanking my luck. 'I came to consult you, or your copy of the Firearms (Amendment) Act Nineteen Eighty-eight.'

'And what is wrong with the office copy?' Mr Munro demanded sternly.

I thought swiftly. 'You borrowed it, sir.'

He waved an impatient hand but relaxed. 'Ask my staff for it back.' In fact, a WPC had returned it to me that morning.

Keith, who knew all about the longstanding animosity between my chiefs which sometimes rubbed off on me, hid his smile. 'How can I help?' he asked.

'Allan Brindle, the keeper at McKimber, has a Chassepot rifle, bored out for use as a four-ten shotgun.'

'True,' Keith said. 'And a useless item it is. I sold it to his boss when the old man was still collecting. So?'

'In the white paper, it was proposed that any such gun reverted to its original status as a firearm.'

'And a damn stupid proposal it was,' Keith said. 'They dropped it before the Act was passed. Whoever proposed it in the first place needed his brains tested.'

'It was proposed by the Committee of Chief Police Officers,' Munro said indignantly.

Keith's smile came again at full strength. 'There you are, then,' he said.

'The rifling could be re-cut.'

'It wouldn't fit any ammunition current today. For the matter of that, any competent mechanic could make an adaptor tube to turn a shotgun into a rifle. Or cut rifling in any piece of iron piping.'

'It's all very well for you,' the Chief Superintendent said sadly. 'You can sell these . . . these killing machines, but I have to deal with the results. As long as the theft of firearms for use in crime is on the increase . . .'

'But it isn't,' Keith said. 'Take a look at the figures for yourself. The civil servants and the police make so much noise about the increase in crimes involving firearms that the media and the public have come to accept it as a fact. But if you look at the Government's own figures you'll see that, over a period during which

26

the total of thefts and burglaries more than doubled, thefts of rifles and pistols dropped and thefts of shotguns remained remarkably constant. And if you try to find out how many of those were later used in a crime, nobody knows.'

Mr Munro finished his coffee, sighed and unfolded his gangling body from the deep chair. 'About the private ownership of firearms,' he said sadly, 'we shall never agree.'

'Did you know that more people are killed by falling trees than by firearms? Wouldn't it make more sense to cut down all the trees instead of trying to stamp out private ownership of guns? Without trees, guns would die out. There'd be nothing to shoot.'

'Now you are being silly,' Munro said.

'Will you look at the figures for yourself and let me know what you conclude?' Keith persisted.

'It would make no difference.' Munro looked at me sharply. 'Are you coming?'

'I want to check Mr Calder's security,' I said.

Keith looked at his watch. 'A long job,' he said. 'You may as well stay to lunch, if Mr Munro permits. Molly will be expecting you.'

Munro looked petulant. He knew that he was being manipulated. But he shrugged. In my reading, he would have liked to be 'one of the boys' but his position and his upbringing combined to set a barrier between him and the coterie which he secretly liked and admired. 'Who the Sergeant cares to associate with in his own time does not concern me,' he said. 'I shall see myself out.'

The door closed behind him.

'He means well,' Keith said. 'Do you really want to look at my security? Again?'

I shook my head. Keith kept a large stock of rare antique weapons in the house. I could only guess at the

27

value and I knew that I was probably underestimating it wildly. His security was the best in the Region.

'Come upstairs anyway,' he said. He called to Molly that I would be staying to lunch and got a cheerful acquiescence in reply. He led the way upstairs and unlocked the steel-backed door to what had once been two large bedrooms, now thrown together to make his workshop and gunroom. Most of the large space was taken up by rack upon rack of guns, each one a collector's piece, but Keith's workbench, with a stool and a visitor's chair, occupied a clear corner. While we talked, Keith settled to work on a handsome Horsley back-action hammer-gun – or so he referred to it. The place smelled of linseed oil.

'What did Munro want?' I asked. 'Or is it none of my business?'

'He tried to pass it off as a social call, but he worked round to asking me whether I thought you were making a proper job of the new shotgun procedures. I said that the new Act was driving a wedge between some police forces and the most law-abiding section of the public but that you were going a long way towards repairing the local damage.'

'Well, thank you,' I said. 'But I don't know that he'll take that as a favourable comment.'

He looked up from a careful inspection of the Horsley's stock. 'He's an old fouter but he's not daft. He can see that some constabularies are alienating the few friends they've got left, and the most influential.' Keith paused, thought for a moment and then decided that we had exhausted the subject. 'What really brings you here? Certainly not to ask me about the status of bored-out rifles. Have you come to ask for my daughter's hand?'

The question was asked lightly but I could sense a

deep anxiety. Keith, by reputation, had been a wild man in his youth; the police grapevine credited him with more recent exploits, most of which I took with a pinch of salt. Whatever the truth, he seemed well aware of the temptations to which an attractive girl could be exposed. I answered him seriously.

'Not just yet,' I said. 'One of these days, when we've learned . . . I nearly said "to live together", but I don't mean quite that.'

'I know what you mean,' he said. 'It takes time to adjust.' He looked happier.

'Would you be pleased if we decided to marry?' I asked him.

He seemed surprised. 'Yes, of course,' he said. 'I thought you knew that. You're right for each other. As right as two people can be, given the great disadvantage of belonging to different sexes.'

It had seemed to me that he was barely aware of my existence. Keith was and is usually preoccupied with the business of the gunshop, his gunsmithing work, some research into gun history and ballistics, occasional investigations of crimes involving firearms and the running of a small shoot which he shared with a few friends and family. Too preoccupied, I had thought, to notice the ebb and flow of his daughter's boyfriends. It seemed, however, that he had not only noticed me but liked me.

That thought led me to another. The note in Mr Brindle's voice and the slight shift of his mouth when he spoke of Ian Kerr had tuned me in to the tiny signals of like and dislike that people unconsciously emit. 'What do you dislike about Allan Brindle?' I asked him.

'I've nothing against him personally,' Keith said. 'He's a good keeper and, for all I know, a good man. Why?'

'Whenever he's mentioned, there's a faint hint of something . . . disdain, I think. If there's a flaw in the character of a holder of shotguns and rifles, it's my job to know it.'

'I don't know him well enough to hold him in liking or dislike,' Keith said after a moment's thought. 'If I looked a bittie po-faced when I mentioned him, it was because of his job.'

'You've always been pro-keeper,' I said, 'always telling us how much better the countryside is for the keeper's attention.'

'I meant it, because it's true,' he said. 'Truer of some than of others. Allan Brindle's a good enough keeper and I think he plays it by the rules – respects protected species, uses legal means for controlling vermin and so on and so forth. But I can't approve of these commercial shoots.' I nodded wisely but he wasn't fooled for a moment. 'In the old days, shooting was by the exchange of invitations. A good shoot was built up over generations by intelligent tree-planting and habitat management. Then came two big changes. Times became harder for the landowner and people became busier and more mobile. A businessman in a big city can't give the time it takes to participate in a shoot. Not to live with it, brood over it, work on it. But he can still have the same instinct to get out in the fresh air in good company and shoot. So he and a few pals book a day at a time on an estate like McKimber. They book for a certain number of birds in the bag and that's what they get, give or take a few, at so much per bird.' Keith looked regretful for a moment and then shrugged. 'But who am I to condemn it? I nearly got on to that bandwagon and made money, but at the last moment I couldn't stomach the misuse of the land. In a way, it's a sort of asset stripping. Nobody cares much what happens to the land just so long as the paying Guns get their money's worth and book again.'

30

'The laird must care,' I said.

'The laird has precious little to do with it. Jeffries, who has the Forth and Clyde Game Farm, runs the shoot. He rents the shooting rights on half a dozen estates, stocks them with birds and lets them for as many days in the year as the stock can stand. And,' Keith said hotly, 'on at least one estate I suspect that he trickles out his left-over birds throughout the season – there's no other way that land could stand up to that amount of shooting. I don't think that Brindle would go along with that, but who knows? – keepers' jobs are scarce these days. The laird at McKimber's no spring chicken and he's had some financial problems. He probably grabbed the money and struck a deal whereby he can hold a shoot or two on his own land for friends and family, with a total bag not to exceed a certain maximum.'

The picture was becoming clearer. If there was no syndicate and the laird's shooting companions were unavailable, Brindle would have to take his chances with the pigeon shooters allotted to his territory.

I repeated what Brindle had told me about his poacher. Keith looked both concerned and amused. 'It happens,' he said. 'Poaching's becoming a way of life with some of them.'

'Surely there can't be much money in it?' I said.

'There isn't. The price of game is nonsensical. The British housewife still prefers a battery chicken, full of hormones and preservatives and salmonella, to a free-range pheasant; and the Continental market's being flooded from behind the Iron Curtain, believe it or not. Money isn't really the objective. And there's no longer a starving peasantry, poaching to survive the winter. In this age of leisure, outwitting the keeper is one of the few kicks left; and if you're careless, the courts are ridiculously lenient over a matter which is in fact theft.'

31

It was rumoured that Keith, in his wilder days, had been a poacher of note; and I thought that I detected a shadow of nostalgia in his voice if not in his words.

'You're probably too young to remember the old Beverley Sisters song. "If there's something you enjoy, you can be certain that",' he sang in a not untuneful voice, ' "it's illegal, it's immoral or it makes you fat." All the same, it shouldn't happen,' he said. Evidently Keith was now on the side of the angels. Perhaps the thrill of the illicit hunt had been replaced by the challenges of business life. 'I might be able to help. If you get a list of all the beaters who've turned out on McKimber over the past few years, and anyone else who could have spied out the land, I'll tell you whether any of them are in the habit of buying airgun pellets locally.'

'I'll do that,' I said. 'Thank you.' Which led me, circuitously, to another question. 'Allan Brindle looked hostile when Ian Kerr's name was mentioned. What does he have against him? Does he suspect him of being the poacher?'

Keith looked up from the tiny scrap of walnut which he was shaping to fill the gap left by a bad chip out of the gunstock. 'Kerr of Miscally?' he said thoughtfully. There was a pause while he sharpened his chisel. 'Kerr gives the impression of being a jolly soul but there's a touch of malice in his nature. Perhaps it's not surprising; life hasn't been altogether kind to him. And Brindle's an uncompromising man. I dare say that a few minutes of reasonable discussion would've resolved the problem.'

'What problem?'

Keith went back to his work. 'I think Ian Kerr owns Miscally outright. Either that or he has a tenancy with sporting rights. Whichever, Miscally isn't part of McKimber Estate. Jeffries has tried more than once to get his hands on the shooting rights. McKimber stands high up but it's relatively flat. You saw how the land drops between the two? Miscally's one of the few places you could put your guns and show them really high driven birds from McKimber. But Kerr's too fond of his own shooting. Instead, he formed his own small syndicate. He plants neips along the McKimber boundary, with pheasant feeders all around. That attracts the birds which Brindle released at great expense to his employer,' he added when he saw that I was only partly comprehending.

'That's quite legal, isn't it?' I said.

'Perfectly legal, though rather unneighbourly. It's often done, but not quite so blatantly. Kerr also made a new pond and feeds it heavily, drawing the ducks from McKimber. Then again, sometimes a runner pricked by one of the guns on Miscally comes down beyond the McKimber boundary. The law says that they can send a dog to fetch it. If the dog's unruly and happens to send a few more birds in the opposite direction . . .' Keith shrugged and grimaced. 'In the end, Allan Brindle got dancing mad. He went to see Kerr and they had the father and mother of a row. I wasn't there, but from what I hear it was a humdinger.' Keith pressed the scrap of walnut into the slot that he had carved for it. It vanished as though the damage had never been there.

I would have delved a little deeper. I was being given a rare insight into the frictions which can exist in the rural fraternity, which meant between gun-owners. But I was distracted by the sound of Deborah's voice below, and shortly thereafter Molly called us down to lunch.

When Deborah was in a room, anyone else present was reduced for me to a mere shadow but I made an effort and paid my hostess proper courtesy. I apologised for having to eat and run. (A two-man team from Edinburgh was due, following up an earlier enquiry about a local burglary, and as the local man I would have to attend them.)

'I understand,' Molly said. 'You have your job. And we're quite used to it, with Deborah. This house is just a hotel as far as she's concerned. Rushing in and rushing out, usually off to some competition.'

'And rushing back with a medal or two,' Keith said. 'She's becoming very good. Don't grumble, be proud of your daughter. Throw your chest out.'

'No,' Deborah said quickly. 'Don't throw it out. I'll have it if you're finished with it.'

I had always considered Deborah to be very prettily endowed in that department, but there was no denying that her mother seemed to have been built on more generous lines. I was grinning all the way back to Newton Lauder.

TWO

Saturday arrived, crisp and clear and with a nip in the air to put colour into cheeks grown pasty during the long winter. No sudden outbreak of crime required my attention; the denizens of Newton Lauder had managed to pass the night with no more than the occasional pub-fight to disturb the peace. For once I was free to take my scheduled day off.

Keith wanted the use of his own jeep and Molly was using the family car, so in mid-morning I picked Deborah up from the shop in the Square. She stacked the back of my car with mysterious bags of different sizes, plus the Labrador that in theory belonged to her father but which was her constant companion.

'You've plenty of warm layers?' she asked as she dropped into the passenger seat.

'Ample,' I said. 'And you?'

'If you could see what I'm wearing underneath these jeans it would turn you off for ever,' she said.

'Try me.'

She put her nose in the air. 'No way. You might come to prefer me that way, and I don't want to be stuck with Dad's longjohns for ever.'

That seemed reasonable. 'I took you at your word,' I said, 'and didn't bring any sandwiches.'

'I've got some. And Mrs Dunbar's very good about

sending Brian out with soup and things to the Guns.'

The wayside branches were white with frost, forming a tracery of amazing intricacy, but the air was too dry to lay ice on the road.

I turned in at the gates of McKimber Estate and drove to Allan Brindle's house. He was digging in his garden, turning over the frozen ground with some difficulty. He had a map waiting for me, with rendezvous points marked and coded. I put the small radio which he gave me into the car, beside the model provided by my employers, and passed on Keith's suggestion.

'That's good thinking,' he said. 'I'll get down to it, as soon as I can.' A shot sounded in the woods and he frowned. 'Which'll not be just yet. I'll need to be getting out and keeping an eye on things.'

'The rest of your pheasants will be getting scattered,' I said sympathetically.

'The further the better. They'll come home again. I'm not afraid of them wandering, except maybe into the game-bags of these beggars.'

'Do you have a note of the dates when the poacher visited you?'

'Aye. There's diary kept. I'll copy it for you.'

I drove back towards Newton Lauder for a mile and then took to a by-road. It led us through farmland of all winter's colours, the brown of plough, yellow-grey stubble, the green of grass and winter barley and the darker green of oilseed rape. My eyes were becoming wiser since Deborah took me in hand.

A small white sign, rather in need of paint, pointed to Nuttleigh's Farm. We dodged potholes and came to the farm buildings – a small farmhouse dominated by the taller barns. The place was unusually tidy for a farm, but there was a faint air of dilapidation as though necessary maintenance had fallen behind. As we got out of the car,

I could hear occasional shots coming clearly through the dry air.

Brian Dunbar was dismantling a tractor engine in the yard. Deborah introduced us and he wiped his hand carefully on what seemed to be half of an old shirt before shaking hands. He was thin and wiry; a dark man, tanned and with a faint blue stubble. In shirtsleeves and bib-and-brace overalls he seemed impervious to the cold, but an ancient tweed cap was pulled down almost over his prominent ears.

'You won't lack for sport,' he said. 'Cushies are here in clouds.'

'Where are they feeding?' Deborah asked keenly.

'Mostly on the barley I lost when the rain began. And there's some rape and some winter barley. Push them off one and they'll go to the other. Your dad's here and that uncle of yours. They've gone by way of Miscally Farm, because they drew March Strip. It didn't please them, but that's the way I aye do it,' he explained to me. 'If I tell them where tae gang, they say I'm no' being fair; an' if I leave them to sort it out for theirselves they a' bunch up in the best bittie. So you draw. There's just the three places left.' He pulled three scraps of paper from a bib pocket and dropped them into his cap, the removal of which revealed a large bald spot and a brow that contrasted palely with his weatherbeaten face. He held the cap above Deborah's head.

Deborah reached up and fumbled for two of the paper scraps. 'Four and five,' she read out.

'Middle Wood,' Dunbar said. 'They'll start coming in there to roost, fourish. You'll get some good decoying until then. That leaves the wee wood, the yin with the high seat, for Ian Kerr. But he'll be busy about his place. Likely he won't show up until afternoon. Until he comes, shoot there if you want.'

'What about yourself?' Deborah asked.

Brian Dunbar smiled for the first time. 'Bless you, lassie, I'll not bother myself. I can shoot here when and where I like. I'm only glad that other folk should spare the time and the cartridges to chase them awa' for a whilie. I'll get on with this dratted job. Since we lost our regular driver the machines don't get their regular maintenance, and there'll be plenty of work for this beggar at the first sign of spring.'

He went back to his tractor, crooning to it as he worked. Deborah hauled bags out of the car. 'If we had the jeep we could have driven most of the way,' she said. 'As it is, we'll have to hump this lot. I call it selfish of Dad. Uncle Ronnie's Land-Rover's off the road again, getting a new flint or something, but he's using an old banger he borrowed from one of his disreputable pals.'

'Then they'd have had to carry their gear,' I pointed out.

'Not necessarily. You can get an ordinary car closer to March Strip by way of Miscally than you can to Middle Wood from Nuttleigh's. Anyway, they're both men.'

Despite the sexism of her last remark, she seized several of the larger bags and set off at a brisk walk along a track in the general direction of the Miscally woods, which I could recognise on the skyline. I followed, toting the remainder. My car would have bottomed on the bump between the wheel ruts.

Birds were on the move. I was seeing the countryside with new eyes. A cock pheasant chortled and took off from some turnips, climbing towards the Miscally woods on their higher ground. I recognised crows – rooks, south of the Border – cruising high and with apparent purpose. I had not been sure that I would know a woodpigeon at a

38

distance and without hearing its gentle, summer call; but I knew with certainty that the birds, smaller than crows, which dotted the sky in twos, threes and larger flocks, bustling with quick wingbeats or dropping in to feed, were our quarry. At any one moment there seemed to be a hundred in the air. Why, I wondered, had I never been aware of the grey hordes?

The track turned a corner and petered out, but there was an open gate and wheel tracks which led along the side of a stubble field. At our sudden appearance a dozen pigeon got up from beyond the next fence and made for the woods. A single shot came back to us. I saw feathers hanging in the air but the birds flew on.

'Missed him,' Deborah said cheerfully over her shoulder. 'They got up out of the barley, so we may get some decoying.' She looked down at Sam, the Labrador. 'If you were a proper dog, you'd carry your share. Or pull a small cart. Perhaps that's why they called them dog-carts,' she added. Sam waved his tail and continued to lead us onward. He knew very well when she was joking.

We crested a small rise. Deborah seemed glad to drop her burden and pause for a moment. I did the same and pulled out Brindle's map to orient myself. Middle Wood, ahead of us, had been fenced against deer and farm animals and seemed to be about three acres of deciduous trees and underbrush. Away to our right, Keith and his brother-in-law were well hidden among the conifers of March Strip, but I saw a pigeon die in the air. The sound of the shot arrived a few seconds later. Beyond Middle Wood I could see the rise of ground to the McKimber woods, but the small wood between, triangular according to the map, was still hidden from me. I remembered looking down on it while I talked with Allan Brindle.

39

'What was Mr Dunbar saying about a high seat?' I asked.

Sometimes Deborah fails to make allowance for my considerable ignorance of shooting and farming. 'Just that there's one in the small wood,' she said. 'The place doesn't have any other name, so that's how he refers to it.'

'Remember that you're talking to an ignoramus,' I said. 'What and why is a high seat?'

She looked at me in faint surprise. 'Roe deer come out of McKimber to feed in the early morning. That's a favourite place for them. The estate lets the stalking. One of the best ways is from a high seat – which is just what it is – so he put one there. You get a great view from up there and the deer don't expect anybody to be up high. And they can't wind you so easily. If he extended the ladder a bit higher,' she added regretfully, 'it would make a great pigeon platform. Like the deer, the woodies don't expect anybody in the treetops, so they either don't see you or else they think they must be imagining you and they keep coming in. If they see you at ground level they sheer away before they come into range. They're the most alert and suspicious of birds, except maybe for crows. Let's move.'

We resumed our burdens and lumbered onward.

At the corner of Middle Wood, we were checked by a barbed wire fence. The wheel tracks turned along the fence and seemed to return along the edge of the stubble on the far side. 'There's a gate along there,' Deborah said, 'but it's miles away – a hundred yards at least. We could drop the bags over and walk round or we could hop over. Sam could jump it but dogs sometimes gut themselves that way. I'll show you a trick that Dad picked up somewhere.'

She took a length of split plastic tubing from one

of the bags. While she fitted it over the top strand of barbs I had time for another look around. In front of us was the great tract of barley which had been spoiled by the rain, a sad sight now, ragged and grey. The smaller wood was in sight, perhaps the length of a football pitch away.

The long scar left after the laying of the water main came from my left, dog-legging slightly to make best use of the contours. Digging and laying had progressed since I had looked down from McKimber. A digging machine stood idle where the backfilling ended at about the mid-point of the nearer side of the small wood; and from there the open trench ran on, finishing near the boundary fence and March Strip. Beyond another hundred yards of spoiled barley was the fence, from which the ground rose steeply to the hedge that sheltered the fringe of the McKimber woods. A trailer, evidently stranded by the excavation, stood forlornly against the corner of the wood. I could make out a rough ladder ascending between the evergreen branches.

'There we are,' Deborah said. 'Now you can swing a leg over without castrating yourself. It would be a pity to lose your whatsits before I've had the benefit. Over, Sam.'

The Labrador, evidently used to the manoeuvre, jumped on to and off the protected top wire. We dropped the bags over and I followed more carefully. Despite her heavy clothing, Deborah vaulted lightly over.

'There's acres and acres of this barley,' she said. 'If we stick together, the birds will just plop down at the other end of the field. We'd better split up. Do you want to squat here or take over the little wood until Mr Kerr turns up?'

'I'm in your hands,' I said.

41

No *double entendre* was intended, but she pretended to recoil like a Victorian maiden. Then she chuckled. 'You'd better not be,' she said. 'I feel a sneeze coming on. Bring your gun and take one of these bags.'

She handed me one bag, picked up another and led me across the field, sticking carefully to a set of 'tramlines' left by the tractor. A stile took us over the fence into the small wood.

'You're in luck,' Deborah said. 'There's a ready-made hide left from last week. Freshen it up a bit while I put out a pattern of decoys. A few lofters placed upstairs may help to pull them.' She took three plastic, full-bodied decoys out of the first bag, tucked them into the front of her jacket and turned to the rough ladder which led up to a narrow platform in a mature pine tree. The hide was tucked under a holly and had been made by lacing grass and twigs into the fence. There was even a plastic oil-drum for a seat. I set about pulling up some dead weeds to thicken the screen.

By the time I was satisfied, the three decoys were perched realistically in the treetops and Deborah had descended the ladder and set up a pattern of decoys in the field. The half-shells had looked unconvincing seen close to but, spread out in a natural-looking pattern and bobbing in the slight breeze, they seemed ready to fly off at the first disturbance. Deborah came back to the fence.

'That should bring a few in to you,' she said. 'If you haven't had any visitors in the first half-hour, pack up and we'll move you. There are some sandwiches in one of the bags, plus a can of beer in case Brian forgets about the coffee. And there are fifty cartridges. If you need more, come to the corner and wave.' She looked at me doubtfully. 'What haven't I told you?'

'If I knew that, I wouldn't need to be told,' I pointed out.

'Indeed?' she said, putting her nose up. 'What is it that I'm always telling you at the clay pigeons?'

'Not to keep dancing around but to pivot on the balls of my feet,' I said humbly.

'See? You know it but you still need reminding. Don't spook the birds by moving too soon. If you get any, set them up in natural positions and start taking in the artificials.'

'What do you mean, "if"?' I protested.

'If you can shoot woodies, you can shoot anything. Clay pigeons don't come suddenly from unexpected angles and jink when they see you. Swing through, take your time but don't hang about.'

'And don't eat with your mouth full,' I said. 'All right, Nanny. I'll be good.'

She put her tongue out at me. 'I'll leave Sam with you. You're more likely to get runners than I am. He'll know what to do. Cheerio!'

She left me to my own devices. I got out some cartridges and unsleeved my gun – a Browning Citori which Keith had sold me second-hand and, I discovered later, at less than a fair price. Sam settled down on my feet. Until Deborah was out of sight and our presence forgotten, I supposed, there would be nothing to do but wait.

Occasional shots now sounded from far and wide as the local Guns took their places. I was facing roughly south-east with the McKimber woods to my right, and somebody there was firing regularly. In front of me, the scar left by the pipe-laying stretched into the distance; but my view in that direction was partly blocked by the trailer which had been backed against the fence nearby. Middle Wood, where Deborah was installing herself, was out of sight behind my left shoulder and beyond a clump of small firs. After a few minutes I heard her first pair of shots. They sounded more confident than I felt.

In my heart of hearts I did not really believe that real birds would be drawn towards these plastic imitations. It was as if aliens had filled a restaurant with plastic people in the hope of ensnaring a few more. The first arrival took me by surprise. It must have settled in the treetops for a cautious reconnaissance, because it dropped suddenly from above my head and landed among the decoys, strolling unconcernedly about with its head and shoulders showing above the rape. I wondered what Deborah would have told me to do. If I shot it on the ground it would be unsporting and I would certainly pepper some of the decoys.

While I was still wondering, a pair of pigeon circled, eyeing the pattern of decoys. It was time to open my account. I fired twice. All three birds streaked off towards McKimber. Whoever was in those woods fired once and I saw a bird fall. I gave myself a mental kick. I had mounted the gun hastily and then hesitated. Deborah's apparently contradictory advice began to make sense.

My next six shots went the same way. I was used to clay pigeons, which follow a predictable path. Their live counterpart, I found, were as likely to be accelerating as slowing and had a maddening knack of jinking suddenly just as I pulled the trigger. Also, being larger, their speed was more difficult to judge.

I pulled myself together, remembered all Deborah's advice and kept still. A singleton approached. I waited until the last moment, mounted the gun and swung through, and the bird dropped dead among the decoys.

That was it. I had killed. As I had expected, I felt compunction. At the same time I felt a surge of pleasure. The hunter had gathered meat and I was no longer a man apart among the Calders and their cronies.

Nearly an hour later I heard the sound of an engine and the trickle of birds cut off. A Land-Rover turned through the gate and followed the earlier tracks around the edge of the field. Brian Dunbar parked just beyond the filled trench and got out. He peered through my screen of herbage.

'Brought you some soup and a hot pie,' he said gruffly. 'May as well take your piece now. You'll get no more customers while I'm here. How've you done?'

'Six,' I said.

He nodded and half smiled. 'For how many cartridges?'

'Quite a few,' I said. I moved my feet to hide the shameful pile of spent shells which had been gathering around me.

'M'hm.' He took a paper bag out of a Marks and Spencer carrier bag and handed it to me and then poured me a mug of soup. The bag contained a hot meat pie. 'I just want to take a look, see whether the ground's settled or frozen enough to bring that trailer across. Then I'll leave you in peace.' He walked off.

His fingers had not been very clean but the pie was delicious and the soup, which seemed to contain every meat and vegetable known to man, was thick and greasy and just what was needed on a frosty day to wash down the pie and a couple of sandwiches.

'No' yet,' Mr Dunbar said on his return. 'I'll give it a day or two. No sign of Ian Kerr? This is his place, mind. When he comes, you'll have to go and join the lassie. I dare say you'll not object to that?' He winked at me and got back into his Land-Rover.

While I waited for the birds to start coming again,

45

I filled my pockets with fired cartridges, leaving an acceptable dozen or so by my feet.

The ruse might fool others, but Deborah had been counting my shots. She appeared beyond the fence a minute or two later with a further supply and a barely concealed grin.

I had an hour to myself after that and I began to get the hang of it. I learned to rise quickly and to get my shot off as I reached my feet, before the pigeon could complete its swerve. Soon I was connecting at least once for every two shots. Sam, who had given me up in disgust, roused himself. Whenever I had a bird down that was not stone dead I gave him a nod. I had found another split tube in one of the bags and fitted it over the top strand of barbed wire, but he could clear the fence in a great bound, ignoring the decoys and dead birds and sweeping up my fluttering victim. Despatching a pigeon, I found, was not as easy as Deborah had suggested; I hated it, but that, I supposed, was the rent I paid for an addictive sport.

The sky emptied again, Sam raised his head and his tail moved. I guessed that another human visitor was on the way; but I never heard a sound until Ian Kerr appeared and climbed over the stile.

'This is your place,' I said. 'I'll clear out.'

'Dinna' fash yersel', laddie,' he said. His accent was much stronger than it had been in the more refined precincts of the Gun Club. 'They'll no' be coming in to roost yet. That's when the sport will be at its best. I'll just sit and look on for a minute.'

He squatted down beside me. Superficially he seemed to be roughly dressed, as men do around farmland, but I noticed that his coat and boots had been expensive. It took me a shot or two before I settled down to shooting beside a more experienced stranger. During the lulls, he

46

chatted in a soft voice, amusingly. He spoke of farming and the weather, and of local personalities; but he never mentioned Brian Dunbar or Allan Brindle by n .e.

During a lull, I asked him whether he could make a guess as to the identity of the poacher on McKimber Estate.

He chuckled and leaned over to give Sam a pat. 'Maybe I could,' he said. 'But I don't know that I'd want to clype to the police. Bird over, coming from your left.'

I fired. The pigeon flew on, apparently untouched, for a dozen wingbeats and then dropped like a stone. 'He's committing an offence,' I pointed out.

'That's not for me to decide. And now,' he said, 'the cushies have stopped moving. They'll start coming to roost soon. You'd better gather your decoys and get back to the Calder lass. You're ettling to wed her, some day?'

'Some day,' I said.

'You could do worse. Yes, you could do much worse.' A sadness in his voice suggested that he had done worse himself.

I picked up the decoys and their sticks, bagged my dead birds and came back to the fence. 'There are three decoys up in the tree by the high seat,' I said.

'Leave them. They'll do some more work yet. I'll fetch them down when it's a' done.'

The bags were heavier. I humped them back the way we had come and found Deborah picking up her own birds and decoys. She had created a roomy hide by draping a net around some young conifers. 'Come and join me,' she said. 'As the light goes we can move and stand among the trees. How many did you get?'

'Nineteen altogether. And you?'

'Forty-something. I should have had more but my

47

fingers were freezing. But you were getting the hang of it,' she added comfortingly. 'I could see birds coming down, just before you moved, which you'd have missed earlier. This turned out to be the better place, that's all. Dad and Uncle Ronnie were having a thin time but they'll get their share when the birds come to roost.'

I tried not to grind my teeth in frustration.

I heard a shot or two from the vicinity of the high seat, but otherwise all was quiet for the moment. 'They're down, having a last feed before they roost,' Deborah said.

Brian Dunbar returned. His Land-Rover stopped just outside the wood and he got out. 'Hungry again?' he asked.

'Give us a chance, I'm still digesting—' Deborah began. 'Keep still,' she said urgently. Dunbar froze.

Four birds sailed in towards the treetops. Deborah fired twice. Two birds collapsed. The other two streaked off towards the high seat. I heard two more shots. One fell and the other flew strongly towards McKimber only to collapse before reaching the trees.

'Nice shooting,' Dunbar said. 'Keith and Ronnie have only got twenty-two between them so far.'

'What happened to you?' Deborah asked me.

'Each time I got on to a bird, you shot it,' I said.

'Well, slap my wrist! Next time, pick the ones on your side of the bunch and I'll stick to mine.'

'I'd better get moving,' Dunbar said. 'Otherwise I'll be spoiling it for everybody. I'll see you again on the way back.' He re-entered his Land-Rover and I saw it head down towards the smaller wood.

The sun was low. The shadows of the tall trees on the higher ground of McKimber Estate were reaching out towards us and the temperature was falling.

A singleton which had been shot at on McKimber

hurried above the fields, saw the Land-Rover, jinked away and came racing towards us. We raised our guns at the same moment but again Deborah fired first, just as the bird jinked again. I was about to take my gun down when I saw that she had missed. I fired, a hasty, scrambled shot, but the bird folded and thumped down in a puff of feathers.

'Well done,' Deborah said. 'That wiped my eye.' She was more generous than I was, but she could afford to be.

'Fluke,' I said.

'I wish Brian would get a move on. Once the movement to roost starts . . .'

'Here he comes,' I said.

The Land-Rover came crawling back but parked at the other end of Middle Wood. From the direction of March Strip a steady thump of shooting came to us. Brian Dunbar approached between the trees carrying a flask and a paper bag.

'Are you ready yet?' he said. 'Coffee and sausage rolls before the real action starts.'

Deborah pulled off her gloves. 'Just what the doctor ordered.'

'Here are your three lofters.' He dropped the decoys beside our bags. 'Kerr says he's finished with them.'

'Thanks,' Deborah said. There was a pause. 'Your Land-Rover will be spooking them.'

'I doubt it. The birds are used to seeing a Land-Rover parked in the fields.' He held out the paper bag but snatched it back. 'Over!'

It seemed that he was right. A small flock was circling. As they headed in to roost I remembered Deborah's admonition. She threw down her gloves. We fired together and two birds dropped. A moment later we heard a shot from Ian Kerr.

'Well done all three!' Dunbar said. He was looking towards the high seat. 'It always surprises me the way you see the bird hit before you hear the shot.'

I looked round but I was too late to see the bird fall. A few feathers hanging in the air at treetop level caught the last of the sunlight.

Dunbar poured coffee. 'Bring the mugs back to the farm. There'll be a dram waiting for you when it gets too dark to shoot,' he said. 'I'll get out of your way now, before the action hots up.'

Deborah raised an eyebrow at him. The crackle of shots from the woods around sounded like a minor war. He grinned lopsidedly at her and turned away. 'Can you come back later and give us a lift back to the car?' Deborah called after him.

'I'll try.' A minute later we heard the Land-Rover grinding towards the farm.

Pigeon were streaming towards their roosts, turning aside at the first shots to seek safer haven elsewhere. The low sun was in my eyes at first but the shadow of the woods soon enveloped us, bringing with it a more penetrating cold. As the light faded, Deborah moved to the other end of the wood and I left the hide to stand against the trunk of a tall pine. My barrels grew warm. I found that I had difficulty seeing my gun against the sky. Paradoxically, my shooting improved.

There was no moon yet. As the last of the sunlight died, darkness was almost complete. Deborah reappeared at my side. 'Time to pick up,' she said. 'I want Sam. There are three down I can't find. I think Ian Kerr's gone home already and I don't hear Dad shooting. We've done well enough for one day.'

While we packed the bags by torchlight Sam circled, bringing back the shot birds two or three at a time in his large mouth. We made one last circuit by the light of Deborah's powerful torch and spotted a wounded bird far out in the stubble, and that seemed to be that. The sound of shooting had almost died away but an occasional shot came from the direction of McKimber and I could see the flashes below the trees. The pigeon had found their way in to roost. I could hear them stirring in the branches above us whenever our noise disturbed them.

Between us, we had more than eighty birds – a considerable weight to add to our bags of decoys, even though these were relieved of the weight of food and many cartridges. 'Brian Dunbar seems to have forgotten us,' Deborah said.

'He only said that he'd try,' I reminded her.

She heaved a bag on to her shoulder. 'He could have tried harder,' she said.

We set off back to the farm, stumbling over unseen bumps. Between the weight I was carrying and the stiffness of a day spent loitering in the cold, the journey was purgatory and I was never so glad to get back to a car. Deborah, I could tell, was near exhaustion, but she never uttered a word of complaint.

We had loaded the car and settled Sam on the back seat when the farmhouse door opened, spilling a long wedge of light. A woman's figure was silhouetted. 'Brian says to come inside for a fly cup,' she called.

We followed her into a large, warm kitchen. The big all-purpose table was pushed back towards the dresser and around the range stood a semi-circle of chairs of various ages and designs. Keith, Ronnie (his brother-in-law) and Brian Dunbar were already lolling at ease.

Mrs Dunbar was in middle age with a figure to match. She could have been modestly attractive but she had made no effort to resist the passing of the years and could now best be described as 'comfortable'. She could be seen to dote on her husband, but evidently she was one of those women who believe that to satisfy the inner man is enough – a belief which often seems to be more than justified. She spoke very little and then only about the food. Her idea of a 'fly cup' included tea – which was virtually ignored, beer and whisky being preferred – with soup, more sausage rolls, bread rolls with savoury fillings and a variety of cakes. After a day in the cold fresh air, I felt half starved. I had promised to take Deborah out to dinner so I tried to hold back, but when I saw that Deborah was eating as though the food would be her last I decided to eat my fill.

'You seemed to be getting the hang of it, towards dusk,' Keith told me.

'I was out of your sight,' I said.

'Even if I hadn't seen you cross the field after Ian Kerr joined you, I'd have known. I could see the birds above the trees, and when I saw that somebody near the high seat was missing at first and then beginning to connect . . . well, who else would it be?'

'That's true,' I admitted.

Keith smiled ruefully. 'Not that we did much better. We picked up about forty between us, but there are probably a few we missed in the dark. We'd better come back by daylight and work the dogs over the ground again.'

'Ian Kerr doesn't have a dog and I didn't see the light of a torch,' Deborah said. 'I bet he's left a few behind.'

'His car's still in the yard,' Dunbar said uncertainly.

Ronnie stirred. He was a large man and his length, sprawled out, seemed to span the room. His face, which could kindly be described as rugged, was puzzled. 'Well, he didn't come past us,' he said. 'No' on the way back.'

'If one of his birds flew on and dropped in McKimber woods,' Dunbar said, 'maybe he detoured around that way. He aye has a bottle in his bag. If he felt he couldn't drive . . .'

'He was sober when I left him,' I said.

'It doesn't take long,' said Ronnie.

'The voice of experience,' Keith said. 'If he'd drink taken, he may have tried to climb to the high seat and had a fall.'

'Likely he's still searching for a lost bird,' Dunbar said. 'But we'd better take a look and see that nothing's come over him.'

'Not that he fired many shots,' Keith said. 'He was doing well at first. Then I saw him miss several in a row and that was the end of it. Maybe he gave up early in disgust and walked home through McKimber. Or maybe not. We'd come down with you, but we can't bide. Molly wanted me back early and Ronnie has a date.'

'How about you two?' Dunbar asked Deborah. 'If Ian's had an accident or a heart attack, I'll need a hand with him.'

Deborah looked a question at me and then nodded. 'We're supposed to be eating out,' she said, 'but after what you've given us it'll be hours before I'm hungry again.'

We thanked Mrs Dunbar and she looked gratified. Outside, the cold attacked my ears and fingers. We piled into Dunbar's Land-Rover. I took the middle seat. Dunbar might have enjoyed changing gear between Deborah's legs but I grudged him the pleasure. The heater soon overcame the cold as we bumped down the track and around the fields.

At the small wood, we disembarked. The moon was beginning to illuminate the cloud cover but the land was dark. Dunbar had a lamp and Deborah her powerful

53

torch. I could see another torch bobbing about on McKimber as a late shooter searched for his birds. There was no sign of Ian Kerr, nor of his gun.

'Did you pick up your cartridges?' Deborah asked. She was using her torch to search in the bushes behind the hide.

'Of course,' I said. She had lectured me on the subject.

'I count eleven here. That's about as many as I heard shots from him. He had more chances than that, though. He must have been feeling poorly.'

We searched the little wood. Dunbar even climbed to the high seat. There was no sign of Ian Kerr. We decided that he must have taken a dram too many out of his bottle and walked home through McKimber woods.

Before we left, Deborah took one last look around the hide. 'What did I tell you to do with your feet?' she asked me.

'To pivot on the balls of the feet and not to dance around,' I said guiltily.

'You forgot, didn't you? From the scrapes you've left, anyone would think that there'd been a struggle in here. Golly, it's cold. Let's go.'

THREE

On the following day, the Sunday, I was off duty again, but Deborah was to be busy, organising a major competition at the Gun Club. I could have gone along for the practice, but claybusting can be expensive and she had made it clear that she would have no time to spare for me.

Keith had asked for my help in gathering up any birds which had been missed in the darkness of the previous night. I wondered what possible use I could be in such a task until I discovered that Deborah had gone off with his jeep and that Molly wanted the family car for one of her ventures in wildlife photography. Like a dutiful prospective son-in-law, if that is what I was, I picked up Keith and his spaniel from Briesland House in mid-morning.

'Sam would have been the better dog,' Keith grumbled as I drove, 'but Deborah's taken him with her.'

'Pity,' I said. 'He enjoys working.'

'Given a free choice, he'd have gone with Deb. The Gun Club members slip him food. He's getting fat. Labs put on weight easily and it's hell's own job to get it off them again.'

'He's a fine figure of a dog,' I said.

Brian Dunbar was working on his tractor again in the yard at Nuttleigh's Farm. He came over to talk

55

while we put on our boots and thick coats. As usual, he was dressed with complete disregard for the weather. Although the sun was out there was no sign of a thaw.

'Agnes Kerr was on the phone,' he said. 'Ian never went home last night.'

Keith straightened up, frowning. 'It isn't quite the first time,' he said.

'It's happened once or twice,' Brian said. 'Once he's drink taken . . . I told Agnes we'd looked for him where he'd been shooting and there was no sign. She walked over and collected his car.'

'Was his gun in the car?' I asked. A man who had decided to go off on a binge was none of my business until he got into trouble. A drunken farmer with a shotgun merited my attention.

'If it was, it was locked in the boot.'

'Have you been down again in daylight?' Keith asked him.

'Just a quick look. There was no sign of Ian. I picked up two birds. I put them in my freezer. I thought you'd not grudge me a brace.'

'Have a few more, if you like,' Keith said.

'I've plenty.'

Keith and I set off. I hoped that we would not find many birds. A single pigeon weighs very little but in bulk, I had discovered the previous afternoon, they can add up to a considerable load. I had had enough of humping heavy weights over the fields.

As we topped the rise and the lower fields came into view, Keith stopped and looked around. 'I can see one already, away over on the grass. I'll get the dog on to it if I can, but a spaniel isn't keen to range so far afield as a Lab.'

I looked where he was pointing but my eyes were not attuned to spotting a fallen bird. By dint of much whistling and many signals, Keith pushed the spaniel further and further out, but I could not see the bird until the dog's head went down and he came sprinting back towards us.

We looped and zigzagged around the fields, paying particular attention to ditches and rough ground. The spaniel did most of the work. Keith had the knack of seeing birds where I could see only leaves or bare ground but, when we came at last to the little wood, I found two in the open trench and then justified my presence by spotting a dead pigeon caught up among the branches of the tree which supported the high seat. Keith went up the crude ladder to shake the bird loose and paused to look around from the high vantage point. I looked in the trailer to see whether a bird had fallen there. It struck me that there was something different about the odds and ends of its load but I was damned if I could think where the difference lay.

'I see one more down in the rape,' Keith said from above. 'And Allan Brindle's watching us from the high ground. I don't doubt he's been doing much the same as us.' I looked up. The keeper was standing like a statue, leaning on his thumbstick. Keith arrived back on the ground. 'Damned if I know where Ian Kerr's got to. Sunk without trace.' He stooped to pick up a few feathers. 'How did you despatch any birds which weren't clean killed?' he asked me suddenly.

'Held them by the body and knocked them on the head with a stick,' I said. 'That's what Deborah told me to do. Why?'

'Remind me to show you how to wring their necks without pulling their heads clean off.'

The spaniel collected the last pigeon, bringing our total to a round dozen.

Brindle had left the edge of the McKimber woods,

pushed through the hedge and descended the slope to the boundary fence. We walked to meet him but Keith diverged from the shortest route to examine the end of the open trench. Brindle waited patiently until we joined him. A polite nod was as much as he could manage by way of a greeting.

'I've this list for you,' he told me without preamble and then switched to Keith. 'Your idea?'

'If that's the list of your beaters and others,' Keith said, 'then yes.'

'It's a good yin.'

Keith took the list out of my hand and fumbled to unfold it with gloved fingers. It ran to about fifty names.

'That many?' I said.

'Aye. There's some can only turn out to beat on Saturdays, others are on shifts. There's four dog/man, two neighbours Mr Jeffries lets shoot rabbit and pigeon out of season, the lad from the game farm who delivers the birds and a pair of foresters who come around lopping the trees. Then there's the laird's gardener.'

'I'll show it to my partner and our two wives,' Keith said. 'They're in the shop more than I am. But I can see two on the list who've bought airgun slugs. Were they two-two or one-seven-seven, did you notice?'

'Two-two, the ones I've found in wounded birds. But that's not to say he doesn't use the both of them.'

Keith nodded. 'There's at least one name I can knock off the list. He bought Derriboots off me a few weeks back. Elevens. He couldn't get his toes into nines. I see that Ian Kerr's listed.'

Brindle's scowl was a thundercloud. 'Aye. He used to come beating. But I fell out with him. If he doesn't want to let his sporting rights, that's up to him, but he's no need to be so brazen about feeding the boundary; and so I told him.'

58

'And Sir Isaac Hendry?'

'I spoke to Mr Jeffries. There's no point doing half a job. Mr Jeffries gied me the names of anybody who's come as a paying Gun more than once or twice and of the laird's usual guest Guns.'

I could see that Keith was hiding a degree of amusement. Looking over his shoulder I could recognise one or two names of men who would have been appalled or frankly incredulous to learn that they had been included in a list of potential poachers.

'I'll see if we can whittle the list down a bit for you,' Keith said. 'Coming back to Ian Kerr, he never went home last night.'

Brindle seemed unsurprised. 'Try the Reaper Hotel. Or the Canal Bar in Newton Lauder.'

'His car was still at Nuttleigh's until his wife fetched it. And I was in March Strip. He didn't go that way.'

'Who knows what a drunk will do?'

'He was sober when he joined me at the high seat,' I said. 'Not even the smell of drink on him. And only an hour or two later, he was gone.'

'A man like that can go through a bottle in an hour, easy. Maybe he came this way.'

'We'd have seen him from March Strip,' Keith said.

Brindle's face twisted in what was evidently a sardonic smile. 'You'd be watching the sky for the next cushie-doo. It's just amazing what a man won't see when he's looking up. I mind once, when I was an under-keeper, one of the Guns was standing with his wife beside him. He was so intent not to be caught napping that when she fell down with a heart attack he never noticed, not until the whistle went for the end of the drive.'

Brindle paused to cogitate, leaning on his thumbstick with the ease of long habit. 'I placed the Guns mysel' and dared them to move. I wasn't having a whole bourach of rogues traipsing around the place. The laird – Mr Youngson – was at the edge of the woods about level with the high seat. Along a bit, about opposite March Strip, there was the man Wright, the one they call Hempie.'

'Uneasy neighbours,' Keith said. I could guess what he meant. 'Hempie' is a Scots word for 'rogue'.

Brindle sniffed and then spat disgustedly. 'You'd think so,' he said. 'I'd not have let him set foot on the land, but it was the laird who wanted me to give him a place and Mr Jeffries said I should oblige him. I was hoping the laird might keep an eye on the wee devil. But I took the wife out for a late drink and when I came back somebody was still shooting by moonlight. I followed the noise and it was Wright. Tried to make out he thought his permission extended to midnight. I soon changed his mind for him,' Brindle said with satisfaction. 'And I made him turn out the postie's bag that does him for a game-bag, but it was all pigeon.

'On the other side,' Brindle nodded towards the south, 'there was a mannie Mr Pollinder had sent. I'd seen him before but I'm damned if I know where. I'm not good at names and faces – they're a' "Hey, you!" to me. I could ask the laird whether he saw Ian Kerr go by.' He was looking at me.

'Don't bother for the moment,' I said. 'Mr Kerr will probably show up in a day or two. You weren't poached last night?'

'Not that I'm aware of,' Brindle said slowly. 'We've finished catching up, so he'd have no chance of robbing the catchers, and with the place hotching with men – some of them stayed on for when the moon came out – he'd be daft to carry an airgun round with him. Mr Jeffries himself was shooting, so I placed him right in the middle of the woods.'

'He won't have seen many pigeon,' Keith said.

'They're his bloody pheasants. We heard a vehicle during the night but I've seen no signs of the poacher.' Brindle paused and scratched his head. 'If our man was a real professional poacher, I'd not have been expecting him on such a night.'

Keith was nodding. 'The clever poacher likes a wind to cover his noise,' he said, 'a night after rain when the birds will be sitting out on the branches so as not to be dripped on, and a starlit night rather than the moon.'

'I jalouse you're not the poacher,' Brindle said. (Keith smiled, not the least offended.) 'You know a little too much. My mannie's not so artful.' He fished out another paper and gave it to me. 'I've looked in my diary and here are the dates he's been at work. Fine nights, most of them. My guess is he's an amateur. But he's slippery.

'Anyway, that's the pigeon-shoot over for the year, thanks be, and from now on anybody found in the woods at night can explain himself. Or he can try.'

We parted company. I was glad to be moving again.

A massive woman – tall, heavily built and with a layer of fat over all – was monopolising the attention of the Desk Sergeant when I arrived for duty on the Monday morning. A few minutes later a message reached me to say that Mrs Kerr had come in to report her husband as a missing person.

Any suggestion that I should see her would have implied that a crime had been committed, yet the suggestion seemed to be implicit. (Later, I recognised it as a cry for help.) But Mr Kerr could have been in hospital following a mishap. He could have gone off to make a new life elsewhere and in other, more delicate, company. Or, as had been suggested by almost everybody who knew him, he might simply be sleeping it off somewhere. On the other hand there was the alternative possibility that he had either committed suicide or been the victim of a crime. I decided to see the lady.

When I met her in a small and bare interview room, I was soon inclined towards the view that her husband could have departed of his own accord. In addition to being large, Mrs Kerr was also both shrill and verbose. Her husband had been adrift for more than thirty-six hours and she wanted to know what was going to be done about it. She agreed that he had stayed away overnight on two or three previous occasions, but never beyond the middle of the succeeding day. He had a fondness for the drink but had never, she was sure, looked at another woman. This was the sum total of her information, but it took her more than an hour to disgorge it. Anxiety takes some people that way.

I tried to explain that there was little that we could do, at so early a date, beyond circulating his name and description. But this was not good enough for the grass widow. She became more voluble and more shrill. In the end, I got rid of her by promising that a search would be carried out. I may have promised that the entire Lothian and Borders Constabulary would combine to comb every pub, ditch and outbuilding in the Region. I would have promised to find him anywhere in the world and to carry him home piggy-back if only that would have induced her to get out of my life for ever.

When I was free at last, I made the necessary report for circulation and then put a more detailed report on our newly acquired fax machine to Edinburgh. A copy would automatically be laid on Chief Superintendent Munro's desk.

I was out of the building for the next couple of hours. An application for a shotgun certificate had been received from a widow who had retained her late husband's gun out of sentiment and as a wall ornament. The 1988 Firearms (Amendment) Act made it clear that no certificate was to be issued if the Chief Constable was satisfied that the applicant had no good reason for possessing a shotgun; on the other hand, it went on to state that 'an application shall not be refused merely because an applicant intends neither to use the gun himself nor lend it for another to use.'

The widow's application seemed to fall into the crack between those two provisions, so I went to visit her. She seemed unimpressed by my argument that a shotgun hanging on two hooks and visible through the nearest window violated the safekeeping requirement in the Act. I had no wish to use my powers under Section 52(3) of the 1968 Act against a well-meaning though misguided widow and confiscate a gun which had been in her husband's family since it was first made. With her permission, I phoned Keith. He listened to my description of the gun and came straight out, bearing a roll of banknotes.

Money talks louder than I do. When we left, Keith was carrying the gun. 'A Churchill "Premier" in almost mint condition,' he said happily. 'I know a man who's been looking for one for years.'

'You'll be able to make his day, and a penny or two for yourself. Mrs Kerr's reported her husband missing,' I told him.

He locked the gun carefully into the back of his jeep. 'I know,' he said. 'Word travels fast in a small area like this. Rumour has it that he's dallying with his fancy woman, but rumour, for once, is mistaken.'

I goggled at him. 'How do you know that?' I asked. 'No, don't tell me,' I added quickly.

'I wasn't going to,' he said. I could tell that he was laughing at me.

'His wife swore blind that he didn't look at other women.'

Keith looked round, but the street was empty. 'He looks damned hard at a waitress in the Quality Café every market day.'

'Do you think the wife doesn't know?'

'She knows all right. She just doesn't want to admit it.'

I leaned back against my car and thought about it. 'If he went off with her, he slipped away from the pigeon-shoot very slickly. Why did you look so hard at the trench? It wasn't to look for dead birds or drunken farmers, because I'd already searched there. And you aren't fascinated by water mains.'

Again Keith looked amused. 'Why do you think?'

'You being you, and Mr Kerr having vanished mysteriously, you probably wondered if somebody hadn't killed him and buried him in the bottom of the trench. But I'd remind you that we saw him shooting after the departure of the last person to be there with him.'

'The last to be seen there,' Keith said. 'Allan Brindle was quite right. You don't see much at ground level while you're waiting for the birds to come in. And it was growing dark soon after that. But the marks of the digger blade's teeth were clear to be seen along the whole length of the open trench. You couldn't fake them.'

My mind caught up and then went a step further. 'But somebody could have used the digger during the night,' I pointed out. 'I don't think that the noise would have reached either of the farmhouses.'

'Then where was he when you went down to look for him?'

'He could have been roughly buried. We wouldn't have noticed in the dark. We weren't looking for the marks of the digger. Somebody used the digger later.'

64

Keith shook his head. 'Uh-uh. The cab and the ignition were locked.'

'But . . .' I was about to mention lock-picking and hot-wiring.

'And,' he said, 'somebody, presumably the driver, had taken the injectors away for cleaning over the weekend.'

That seemed to be that. 'So he definitely left the area,' I said.

'Leaving a mystery behind him.' Keith thought about it and then shrugged. 'The ground was too hard to accept ordinary footprints. And by now the area will be hopping with pipe-fitters and labourers, with all their vehicles, not to mention the digger churning up the area. If Ian Kerr doesn't turn up alive, you're going to have a problem.'

'He'll be sleeping it off in his girlfriend's bed.'

'If you say so.' He took a neatly tabulated printout from his pocket and gave it to me. 'I put Brindle's list on to the word processor together with such data as Wallace and Molly and I could remember between us. He's going to ask Janet – she has a memory like an elephant – and take a look through the shop records. We may come up with some more.'

I glanced at the list. About eight of those listed had bought airgun pellets and there were some notations about boot purchases, but against most of the names there was still nothing. 'I hope so,' I said. 'I'd like to show Allan Brindle that the police can be on his side, but there are a hell of a lot of suspects.'

'Potential suspects,' Keith corrected me. 'I wish you joy of them.'

I could guess at his meaning. A long list of suspects remained. Most of them were local characters of the rougher sort, who could be expected to lie to keep each

65

other out of trouble; the remainder were, or should have been, above suspicion.

I called in at the Reaper Hotel and drove on again to the Canal Bar, a lowly pub where they do a surprisingly good bar lunch. Ian Kerr was well known at both, but at neither did the staff or such regulars as were present remember seeing him on the Saturday night.

There was a note on my desk directing me to phone Superintendent McHarg forthwith if not sooner. But the phone rang before I could lift it. I picked it up irritably. Mr McHarg had a maddening habit of ordering you to do something and then doing it himself.

But it was Chief Superintendent Munro on the line. 'About this morning's report,' he said without preamble. He never announced his identity. He had no need to do so. His lisping, lilting, Hebridean voice was enough identification. 'I didn't know that we had an outbreak of poaching.'

'Nor did I, sir,' I said. This seemed to be a propitious moment for the grinding of axes. 'It hadn't been reported. Some of the landowners have stopped bothering. Too many officers treat poaching as a prank or as a justifiable gesture against grasping landlords. I'm trying to change their attitude.'

'Quite right. Poaching is for the police to deal with. The last thing we need is an affray between poachers and keepers. This is a matter of crime prevention if ever there was one. Concentrate on it. If anything relevant to the farmer Kerr should turn up, we can think again. Until then, put him on the shelf. The man's a notorious drinker. He'll very likely turn up in due course, just as he has in the past, very ashamed of himself and apologetic that his wife bothered us.'

Which was all very well, but when I phoned Superintendent McHarg his view was diametrically opposite. 'Poaching with an airgun,' he said disgustedly. 'Boy's mischief! Time enough to worry about it when the keeper catches the culprit. If then. The keeper can give him a hot arse and we mustn't. The disappearance of a man of property under the nose of one of my officers is much more serious. A farmer doesn't drop out of sight for nearly forty-eight hours because he's had a few drinks. Not unless he's collapsed in a ditch. You've checked the local hospital?'

'Not yet, sir,' I admitted.

'Do it right away. He may have had an attack, felt it coming on and wandered off in search of help. Make some enquiries. Be ready to show that we made an effort, just in case he's found dead of hypothermia. Get on with it.'

He hung up on me before I could agree or disagree.

A minute's thought satisfied me that Mr Munro had every right to tell me to tackle the poaching and none to instruct me to forget about the disappearance of Ian Kerr. Of Mr McHarg, the reverse was true. But, because the two cases covered the same territory and some of the same people, they could be handled in parallel; and if either of my superiors objected they could argue with each other and leave me out of it. Not that they would, but they could.

I phoned the local hospital and the two others within easy reach. For once Superintendent McHarg had not beaten me to it. None of them had admitted Ian Kerr nor anybody of his description. The only dead body so far unidentified, a road accident victim, was female.

A starting point common to both cases would be the laird, Mr Youngson. (In Scotland, the owner of the land and the biggest house may be known as 'the laird', whether duke or commoner.) I phoned McKimber House, expecting an argument with a butler at least, but the phone was answered by a surprisingly young voice which identified itself as belonging to Mr Youngson. He agreed to see me later in the afternoon without showing the least curiosity as to what I wanted of him.

Another loose end was the lady friend. I called in at the Quality Café. The only waitress visible was dark and Keith had said that the subject of Ian Kerr's interest was blonde. The manageress was dealing with invoices in a tiny cubbyhole. When she invited me inside there was no room for either of us to sit but she seemed to enjoy the propinquity – more than I did, for her perfume would have made a good shark repellent.

Deirdre Watson, the blonde waitress, was off duty until six. The news of Ian Kerr's disappearance had already done the rounds. As tactfully as I could, I explained that Deirdre Watson might be able to help me with my enquiries. The manageress seemed amused, doubtful, reluctant and not unpleasantly scandalised, but after a little persuasion she gave me Ms Watson's address. This was in a block of old, tenement flats in the least salubrious corner of Newton Lauder.

I climbed a stone stair between walls which showed signs of damp, and knocked on a panelled door badly painted in a dark brown. I could hear soft sounds from beyond the door but there was no answer. I knocked again.

'Who's yon?' demanded a woman's voice throatily.

'Detective Sergeant Fellowes.'

There was a pause. I could hear whispering. For some reason, I thought that one of the whisperers was a man. 'How do I know you're who you say?'

'If you'll open the door I'll show you my identification.'

The door opened a crack and a brown eye, heavily made up, examined my card, flicking to and fro between the photograph and my face. A waft of overheated air came out to meet me.

'But what the de'il are you needing me for?' she asked irritably. Evidently she had detected some resemblance between my face and the passport-type photograph. I was less than flattered.

I had come to ask rather than to answer, but her question seemed a fair one. 'I'm looking for Ian Kerr.'

'He's no' here. I've no' seen him for a week or mair.'

'I want to see for myself.'

'You can bugger off,' she said elegantly and tried to close the door.

I decided that Deirdre Watson was not the type to bother with the formalities of the Complaints Procedure. We each had a foot against the door, but mine was in a heavy shoe while hers, as I discovered, was bare. I got my arm into the gap and levered. She resisted while calling me some names which had definitely not figured on my identification and then gave up the unequal struggle.

The door swung open.

Ms Watson, clad only in some scraps of cheap nylon, was framed in an untidy room. In the background Ronnie, Molly Calder's brother, was struggling hastily into a pair of grey longjohns. An awesome sight.

'I telled you Mr Kerr wasna' here,' Ms Watson screeched.

Ronnie was less angry than he was anxious. 'You'll not tell Molly?' he said.

Backing out, I said that I would not. As I went to the car with my ears burning, I decided that I had learned one thing. I now knew why Keith had been so sure that Ian Kerr was not recovering from his excesses in the arms of Deirdre Watson.

* * *

69

Whoever built McKimber House in the late eighteenth or early nineteenth century had avoided the worst excesses of Scottish Baronialism and had even restrained himself in the matter of size. The result was a pleasant country-house no larger than a medium-sized hotel. The weathered stone would be fuzzy with Virginia creeper in summer and blazing with it in autumn, but in late winter the bare stems looked like wandering cracks. The sash and case windows were in need of paint – one of these days, the laird was going to be faced with the cost of new sills.

The maid who admitted me was the same middle-aged and very plain woman who had directed me to Allan Brindle's house. She wore a thick cardigan over her uniform. The reason for this departure from strict form was obvious as soon as I realised that the house, which had seemed hot when I came in from the bitter outdoors, was not even warm. The rooms were well provided with radiators, but these were doing no more than protecting the house against damage by frost. Presumably the thermostat was turned well down. The cost of heating such a place in such weather would have crippled most purses.

Mr Youngson was waiting in a library which was only half filled with books and which smelled of must. A log fire in the grate was doing little more than pull a draught across the room.

Despite his voice, the laird was a man in his sixties, thin and spry but with grey-white hair thinning at the back. His face was lined but was both tanned and ruddy, as though he spent most of his days in the open air. He seemed rather bulky for his build and his tweed suit fitted tightly. This, I realised, was not because he had put on weight; he could be seen to have dragged his jacket on over several thick sweaters.

A large coffee-pot was murmuring to itself on a corner table. This turned out to contain soup. He offered me some but I declined. He selected a large mug from among several others and helped himself, taking a stand in front of the fireplace and cupping the mug in his hands. 'You won't mind,' he said. It was not a question. 'Only way to keep warm in this barrack of a place. You'd better keep your coat on. If I turn the thermostat any higher, the boiler can go through a tankful of oil before the fabric of the building has begun to heat. The best I can do is to try to survive until spring. What did you want to see me about?'

The chair which he offered me was a huge, leather affair and very cold. I went and stood beside the radiator, which was at least faintly warm. 'You know that Mr Kerr, of Miscally Farm, has disappeared,' I began.

'No,' he said, 'I didn't. Nobody tells me a damn thing. I'm a long way off the main stem of the grapevine. Done a bunk, has he?'

My stance by the radiator was in the downdraught from a window. I joined him at the fireplace. 'Not that we know of,' I said. 'Why would you think that?'

'He's an abrasive character at times,' Mr Youngson said slowly, 'and he can put people's backs up. Don't mistake me,' he went on more briskly, 'if he likes you, or if things are going his way, he can be good company. I get on well with him. A bottle to him at New Year and a favour in return, that sort of thing. But that didn't make him any other friends.'

'How was that?' I asked. Any background information can prove useful in the end – or a total waste of time.

'When I held my own shoot . . . Would you believe that I'm only allowed to shoot over my own land once a year, maximum a hundred birds and under Jeffries' keeper's directions?' For the first time his voice, which had been almost jocular while he was speaking of his tribulations, became indignant. He sighed. 'But that was the nature of the agreement and I suppose I have to abide by it. Anyway, Ian Kerr gave me permission for my guest Guns to be placed on his land, below the highest part of my ground. We made it the last drive and showed them some splendid birds,' he said with animation, 'real archangels. But Ian never let Jeffries do the same for his paying Guns and that got right up Allan Brindle's nose.' The laird sounded not displeased.

'That doesn't explain why you thought that he might have "done a bunk",' I pointed out.

He frowned. 'No, it doesn't. But I had the impression that Ian was getting fed up with his life. Money problems – the bottom's dropped out of farming lately and don't I know it? I'm just squatting here and waiting for my son to make his pile and come home to take over. Not that Ian's as badly off as some of them around here. He owns Miscally and he's a thrifty farmer. But to add to money trouble, they have a mentally handicapped son. Mrs Kerr manages to cope with him, but she won't let Ian say a harsh word to the boy, not even when he set fire to the barn. It gets on top of Ian at times and then he takes to the bottle. Do we know what happened to him? I suppose not, or you wouldn't be here.'

'He was last seen on the pigeon-shoot, the day before yesterday,' I said. 'He was in the small wood where the high seat is. Nobody saw him leave. You were the nearest Gun in McKimber woods, I believe. What did you see?'

Mr Youngson filled a large pipe and lit it while he thought back. He cupped the bowl of the pipe in his hands, as he had the mug of soup, in search of a little extra warmth. 'Not a whole lot,' he said at last. 'I was facing that way, watching for them coming in to roost, and you don't look around a lot when you're shooting. I didn't even know who was placed down there. Let's see, now. I got to my position after lunch, between two-thirty and three. It was bloody cold but at least there were some birds about and I had an excuse to shoot on my own patch. I glanced towards the high seat once, during a lull, and a man with a black dog left the small wood and walked up towards Middle Wood. Ian Kerr doesn't have a black dog, just collies for the farmwork. Is that any help?'

'That was me,' I said. 'Go on.'

'You shoot, do you? Perhaps next season . . .' He looked at me with more interest but decided not to pursue that subject for the moment. 'I take it that you left Ian in place, because somebody was still shooting there – and doing it damned well. I wish I could still shoot like that. I used to be a not-bad performer but my co-ordination seems to have gone to hell. I only picked eighteen birds for two boxes of cartridges. Boxes of twenty-five,' he added sadly. 'Woodies are a far cry from pheasants.'

'They're a far cry from clay pigeons,' I said. 'I don't think that I did any better. What did you notice after that?'

'Nothing until – let's think – yes, until my attention was caught by the sound of Brian Dunbar's Land-Rover coming from the direction of March Strip. One thing about the Dunbars, if you're shooting on their farm she sends him down with hot drinks now and again. If the flow of birds hadn't dried up then, the disturbance would have put them off.' He paused, looking puzzled. 'Funny thing, I could see a bit of the ladder that goes up to the high seat and I saw somebody climbing up.'

73

'He was taking down some decoys from the treetop,' I said.

'Lofters, eh? Wish I'd thought of that myself. Might have encouraged the beggars to come a little closer and slow up a bit. Some little while later, the Land-Rover went up towards Middle Wood. Taking you your dummies and a share of the grub?' (I nodded.) 'After that . . . yes, it's coming back to me. The pigeon had made up their minds that they were coming in to roost and there was a lot of shooting. But I only heard a few more shots from the direction of the high seat. And then they stopped. I knocked off soon after that. Must've been about five. The light was going, and anyway I was feeling the cold. All that I wanted in the world was a hot bath and a large gin-and-nothing.'

'You saw nobody entering or leaving the small wood? Other than Mr Dunbar?'

'Nobody at all. But I wasn't looking,' he repeated patiently. 'Most of the time, I was watching the sky or keeping an eye on such birds as were in sight to see whether they were going to come my way. You must know how it is.' He hesitated. 'You're considering the possibility of what they call "foul play"?'

'Along with sudden illness, brainstorm, suicide or just plain going away,' I said, 'yes.'

'I'm not saying that anybody did away with him. But they might have done. And if so . . . Have you had a good look at the bottom of the trench? It would be easy for somebody to dump him in the bottom of the trench beside the pipe where the backfilling stopped and shovel some earth over him. In which case, he's probably ten feet down by now. I saw the men back at work this morning.'

I blessed Keith for his thoroughness. 'The marks of

the digger blade were visible all the way along,' I said. 'And the digger itself was immobilised.'

'That seems conclusive,' he agreed. 'So much for an amateur attempt to be helpful. I'm sorry.'

'Don't be sorry,' I said. 'I need all the brain-power I can borrow. We went back to look for him that evening, but if his mortal remains are still around I can't imagine where. So either he walked off or somebody came and removed him. Either way, I'll have to speak to your neighbouring Guns. I believe that a man named Wright, known as Hempie, was one of them?'

The laird thought and then nodded. 'He was about a hundred yards to my left as I looked towards Nuttleigh's. Funny wee chap. Uses a hammer gun older than himself, and he's no chicken.' He hesitated again, as though about to make a shameful admission. 'I know him quite well. I wouldn't trust him very far, but I like him. We're as different as chalk and cheese and yet we enjoy the same things. But you may have a job getting hold of him.'

'How's that?' I asked.

'He lives out of the back of an old van and goes wherever he can get a bit of casual work about the farms or pick up some money without too much effort. Hedging, ditching or helping with the harvest, that sort of thing. In short, he lives the kind of unencumbered life I sometimes hanker for.' Mr Youngson gave a quick snort of laughter at his own folly. 'Don't suppose I'd enjoy it in reality. But I've left instructions that whenever he wants a bath or a chance to do some laundry he has the freedom of the servants' quarters. He likes to keep himself clean and as far as I know he's never yet abused my hospitality. I'll tell them to contact you next time he shows up, shall I?

'On my other side, Brindle placed a man I didn't

know. I spoke to him when I went to collect a bird. Big chap, quietly spoken, not very talkative, local accent. He had a newish gun, an over-under, one of the cheaper ones. That's about all I can remember about him. If Brindle doesn't know who he is, you could probably get his name from that chap Pollinder at the Gun Club.'

'Yes.' I thought over what had been said. 'Did they both seem to be shooting steadily, or were there long pauses?'

'Who knows? There would be pauses between incomers as there always are. When the birds are coming in, you don't pay much attention to where other shots are sounding from.'

My buttocks were singeing. I turned round to face the fire. 'I'll put it another way,' I said. 'When you're watching for birds, you tend to watch the ones which fly over somebody else's position, because any which are missed may swerve in your direction. If they don't get shot at, you wonder why not. Did you notice any such indications that one of your neighbours might have moved away from his position?'

There was another pause for thought, a longer one. 'In those circumstances,' he said at last, 'I think I'd assume that the other chap was having a pee or a coffee, or hadn't reloaded, or had forgotten to put off his safety catch, or had left his position to gather his shot birds, or the sun was in his eyes. The only time I was surprised to see a pigeon go over unsaluted, it had flown over the high seat. But that was late on, when the light was failing and I was thinking of packing it in, so Ian might already have left or been removed. On the other hand, he might have decided that the light was too bad for him.'

It was beginning to look as though Ian Kerr could have ridden off on a camel without attracting any attention, provided only that the pigeon were presenting tempting

76

targets at the time. I could only hope that when he turned up, alive or dead, the circumstances would be self-explanatory. Neither testimony nor mute evidence was going to solve the mystery of his disappearance.

But if Mr Youngson had quitted the scene early, Ian Kerr might have left or been removed past the position he had vacated. 'Who was behind you?' I asked him.

'Steven McAlistair was somewhere behind me and to my right. He shoots regularly here with Jeffries. It must cost him an arm and a leg,' the laird said enviously, 'but he can't plan too far ahead so it suits him to grab a place at short notice when it's available, rather than join a syndicate and find that he's busy whenever they have a shoot planned. He's manager of Landig Plant Hire.

'Straight up the ride behind me there was a young man I didn't know although I've seen him in more than one context. He must shoot sometimes with Jeffries, because once or twice on shoot days I've seen him arrive on foot with a gun and a game-bag slung over his shoulders. So he lives locally and either he walks here or somebody drops him at the gates. But I've seen him somewhere else, I'm damned if I know where.'

There were other questions which I should have asked, but my options of freezing in a polished leather chair or continuing to stand at the fireplace, rotating like an ox on a spit to avoid being roasted on one side and frozen on the other, and with a ferocious draught chopping me off at the ankles, were each looking ever less attractive. I wanted to finish the interview, resuming it, if necessary, in my cosy office. But I also wanted to discuss poaching. A happy inspiration visited me.

'You've been very helpful,' I said. 'I'll come back to you if I think of any more questions about Mr Kerr. Let's change the subject. We've had a complaint of regular poaching on your land.' I patted my pockets.

'I seem to have left a paper in the car. Perhaps we could go out to it for a minute.'

'If you wish.'

It was still daylight. The days were beginning to draw out although spring was still only a distant dream. As we walked into the colder outdoors I managed to fumble the list out and hold it out of sight, producing it as if from the door pocket as we got into the car. I started the engine, which had not had time to cool completely, and turned up the heater. Beautiful warmth seeped around the interior along with the reek of the laird's tobacco.

Mr Youngson held his hands towards the outlet. 'That's better,' he said. 'This is luxury. How can I help? I've heard nothing about any poaching.'

'Probably not,' I said. 'Mr Brindle's been very quiet about it. He seemed to have despaired of getting real-istic help from the police. He was trying to keep watch himself but he's never quite managed to come up with the poacher. I've persuaded him to accept help from the proper authority.' I opened up the paper. 'This is a list. Not suspects, you understand – just a list, as comprehensive as we can make it, of men who might know the ground well enough to evade Brindle at night. We're looking for somebody who takes a size nine boot and wears ordinary wellingtons at least some of the time. He takes a small dog with him. Possibly a pipe-smoker.'

He turned in his seat and looked at me in surprise. 'Has Brindle smelled tobacco on these occasions?' he asked me.

'He didn't say so. He's found used matches but no cigarette-ends.'

Rather ostentatiously, I thought, Mr Youngson ap-plied a gas-lighter to a pipe which was already burning well. 'There are poacher's tricks which could require a match. Burning sulphur, for instance. Let's have a look at your list.'

I backed the list with a road atlas and held it against the dashboard. Mr Youngson took one look and then gave his disconcerting snort of laughter. 'Not that I give a damn about Jeffries' pheasants,' he said. 'We can reduce the list somewhat.' He pointed with the stem of his pipe. 'Poor old William, my gardener, he's half blind and his night vision is nil. And this old boy's in a wheelchair – he has an electric vehicle to take him about on the shoot and he shoots from its seat. And this one's known locally as Bigfoot.'

When he had finished and I had jotted down the outcome from his remarkable store of local knowledge, another nine names on the list could be tentatively discarded. 'I'm very much obliged to you,' I said.

He shrugged and prepared to get out into the cold. 'I'd like this poacher to be discouraged before my son makes his pile and I take the shoot back from Jeffries,' he said.

FOUR

Sam Pollinder had recently moved house to be nearer to the Pentland Gun Club, but Deborah had his new phone number and I called him at his home next morning. He had heard about the disappearance of Ian Kerr and was inclined to take it more seriously than did others in the neighbourhood. 'Mr Kerr can go off the rails sometimes,' he said. 'Not surprising, considering. But he'd never run off.'

'Considering what?' I asked.

'He has his troubles. Don't we all?'

'I'm having some at this moment,' I said in a sudden burst of irritation. 'Everybody hints at Ian Kerr's personal problems but nobody ever gets around to telling me what they are.'

'I'm sorry. It's the sort of thing that gets talked about in whispers if at all, for the family's sake. It's the boy. It never occurred to me that you wouldn't know, although they keep very quiet about it. The Kerrs have a handicapped son. Years ago, Ian tripped and fell with the baby in his arms. The boy was brain damaged. Ian got pissed out of his mind when we were alone in the club one evening and cried on my shoulder, metaphorically speaking, for more than an hour. I suppose that's one of the reasons why I'm shy about discussing it – one tends to respect the confidences of a drunk. There's no doubt that he still has a deep sense of responsibility. He might well want to run away, but he wouldn't do it.'

'I'll be damned,' I said. A dozen small contradictions were explained. 'When you talk about going off the rails . . .'

'Drink,' Sam said. 'And he could suddenly blow his top over some trifle. Also, sometimes, women. But that was nothing serious. He poured it all out to me – said that his wife had been a wonder with the boy, he couldn't praise her enough, but that she had no time for him as a husband any more. That much would be true, but it seemed to me that the disenchantment was mutual. His wife would have been a handsome woman in her day – not that I knew her then,' Sam added hastily, as though I might suspect him of nursing a lingering passion for Mrs Kerr, 'but large women can't afford to run to seed and I don't suppose he fancies a wife built like the proverbial brick whatsit. He has the same needs as any other man, perhaps more than some, so he sought relief with more accommodating women. That just added to his sense of guilt. He never formed a relationship, as they say. You can take it from me that he didn't run off. Something's happened to him. How can I help?'

'You probably know how we were positioned,' I said. 'Mr Kerr was shooting in the small wood with the high seat. Deborah and I were to the east of him and he didn't leave in that direction. Deborah's father and uncle were in March Strip to the north. If anyone had come or gone by the south, I think we'd have seen him. We went up to the farm when the light failed and he may have left while we were there. When we went back to look for him, an hour later, there was no sign of him. Somebody who stayed on later than we did may have seen or heard something; and there's the possibility that he went, or was removed, by way of McKimber Estate. Who did you send there?'

'Not many. Five, I think. Let me look at my notes.' I waited on the line while the sound of rustling papers came over the wire. I eased the receiver away from my ear, which had grown hot during Sam's long exposition. 'Yes, five. The arrangement, as always, was that farms and estates had the first call on their own land and they'd let me know how many extra Guns they could accommodate. The McKimber keeper phoned me before the first day, to tell me that they could cover all their own woods. Then he phoned again to say that five Guns couldn't or wouldn't turn up for the second Saturday.

'The exercise gets complicated because of groups of odd numbers who want to shoot together. Rather than re-do the whole draw, I moved the five who'd been on Nuttleigh's Farm first time around and started to fill Nuttleigh's again.'

'Who were the five?' I asked.

'I couldn't put names to them all. Steven McAlistair, the plant hire contractor, asked for five places. I pulled Nuttleigh's out of the hat for them. He swore that they were all safe and well behaved, so when the McKimber keeper – Brindle, is it? – when he seemed to be getting anxious about who was being sent to his patch, I moved them as a group. I believe that Andrew Nairn was one of them,' Sam added in the tones most commonly used for the dropping of names.

The name meant nothing to me, except that it was on Allan Brindle's list. 'I'll get on to Mr McAlistair,' I said.

'Walk on tiptoe,' Sam advised. 'He has a short fuse.'

I thanked him, disconnected and phoned Landig Plant Hire. Mr McAlistair's secretary was protective but she relayed a message to him and came back to say that he was going out to Nuttleigh's Farm. I said that I would meet him there.

The thermometer insisted that the day was warmer than its predecessors although a fresh breeze made me glad of my sheepskin coat. Dark clouds were banking up to the west. Even in the middle of the morning most drivers were showing lights and probably wishing that they lived somewhere much further south.

I approached the site of the pipe-laying by way of McKimber Estate. I could bring the car closer to the work that way, saving myself the long hike over Nuttleigh's, and I might well want to see Allan Brindle again. I parked the car where I had left it on my previous visit. Andrew Nairn, whoever he might be, had carefully gathered up his empties but I saw a black Express cartridge where his ejector had tossed it and where, presumably, he had missed it in the darkness. I walked to the edge of the woods.

The excavation had progressed past March Strip and into Miscally land but the digging machine had returned and was backfilling the trench just beyond the small wood. If Ian Kerr failed to return alive, and if none of the witnesses had seen him depart, the search for his body was going to be an expensive business. Men were working on the pipes in the open section, but I could see a trio grouped in discussion and struggling to control large sheets of paper in the strengthening breeze. A Range Rover stood nearby and I looked at it with envy. Given a vehicle like that, I could save myself a great deal of plodding around in muddy fields. I found a gap in the hedge and slithered my way down the steep slope to the boundary fence. The discussion seemed to be finishing. Plans were being folded. One of the men saw me and walked in my direction.

84

'Mr McAlistair?' I asked.

'That's me.' He was short and thickset with a round face centring on a small, black moustache. His coat and what I could see of his trousers looked expensive and much too fine for squelching around among excavations, but the effect was marred by black wellingtons and a safety helmet. 'You'd be Sergeant Fellowes?'

I said that I was.

'You wanted to ask me about Saturday afternoon? Go ahead, then.' His manner was brisk and businesslike to the point of being overbearing.

'Mr Kerr, the farmer at Miscally, was last seen in the little wood there,' I said. 'That would have been between three and three thirty on Saturday. By six, he had vanished without trace.'

'Well, I can't help you,' he said. 'I had to leave around five, when the action was just warming up. And I was placed well back in the woods. Never saw anybody moving around except the Guns. Hardly saw a pigeon either. That all? It's a cunt of a day. Let's get this over.'

'You brought a party of five,' I said, 'including yourself. Who were the others?'

He glared at me, as though about to ask whether I suspected one of his guests of making away with the farmer. A moment's thought must have convinced him that the question was reasonable. 'Andrew Nairn was one,' he said. Again there was that suggestion of name-dropping.

I looked the question at him.

'Andy Nairn. Surely you've heard of the Edinburgh Rock?'

I wasted several seconds in trying to associate the name with the rock on which Edinburgh Castle stands. Then I made the connection. 'Andy Nairn the rock singer?'

85

'Yes, of course,' he said impatiently. 'We've done some business together so I asked him along. He bought Tundle House, just over a mile from here – more for his parents than for himself, although it's his home on the few occasions when he's not on tour. He was at the other end of the ride you've just come down. The others were employees of mine.' He waited for me to finish scribbling. Evidently he was well used to giving dictation. 'Two of them, my surveyor and the accounts clerk, wanted to be together, so the keeper placed them in a clearing right over at the far side of the woods. They won't have seen anything.'

'That leaves one more,' I said.

'Ron Campbell,' he said. His brash manner showed a trace of what might almost have been embarrassment. 'He might be able to help you – he was placed somewhere over this side.'

'Is he a large, rather silent man with a local accent?'

'That sounds like Ron.'

'He's the one I most wanted to see,' I said. 'If I'm right, he was positioned at the edge of these woods.'

Mr McAlistair fell silent. I thought that he was waiting for me to speak and yet I waited. There was something in the air. 'Ron's always seemed to be a good man,' he said suddenly. 'In the normal way of things, he'd never harm a soul. I just hope he hasn't done something stupid this time. I'll tell you this. It's better that you hear it from me than in the form of a garbled rumour.' He fell silent again.

'Go on,' I said. 'I won't jump to conclusions.'

'You'd better bloody not!' he said. 'But Ron . . . Ron used to work for Ian Kerr, partly. The way it was, the two farms, Miscally and Nuttleigh's, they came to an agreement years ago about sharing machinery. Leased some of it from me, bought the rest on a bank loan. Ron worked for the pair of them, driving and maintaining the combine, the drier, the tractors and all the ploughs and harrows. But he came to me one day, when I was looking for a driver. He didn't say much, but I gathered that Kerr had lost his temper over something trivial and Ron was damned if he was going to put up with it. For one thing, when Ian Kerr takes a scunner he doesn't let go of it in a hurry. He likes a peaceful life, does Ron. He took a scunner of his own, to Kerr. Swore he'd never set foot on Miscally again.

'So I took him on. He's the best digger driver I've ever had. I've seen him, for a bet, toss a golf-ball out of his bucket and into a hat. In fact, I won money on him. Just over there, it was.' McAlistair jerked his head towards the pipe-track.

The suddenness of the information almost took my breath away. 'You mean, he's the driver of the digging machine down there?' I said. 'I'd better go over and speak to him.'

The small moustache lifted in what might have been a smile or a sneer. 'You'll have a long walk. He's taken his wife away to Spain on one of those cheap winter packages. He was driving the digger here until Saturday morning. They left for Gatwick on Sunday. I think he chose the date so as to miss out on Miscally.'

'Who was his travel agent?'

'How the hell would I know?'

'When do you expect him back?' I asked.

'Not for another ten days. Kerr will surely have turned up by then. You'd much better go and speak to Andy Nairn. The keeper put him at the other end of that ride you've just come down.' He looked up at the sky. 'Snow's coming soon. Ron may have made a bad guess. If the weather holds us up on this job, we may still be on Miscally ground when he gets back. Is that the lot? I have more to do than stand around talking.'

'One more question,' I said. 'Does Ron Campbell usually take away the injectors for cleaning?'

'Often, yes. Always, if he saw black smoke at the exhaust. Very fussy about machinery is Ron. I noticed on Saturday that he'd removed them. I meant to mention it to him but I forgot; and on Sunday night I had a sudden picture in my mind of him going off to Spain with the injectors in his pocket. But I wronged him. I checked on Monday morning and they were back in place. That's your lot.'

He turned and stumped away without giving me a chance to confirm that I had finished with him. When he began to cross the soft backfill he began to sink into the mud. He made the mistake of slowing down, became bogged and walked out of one of his wellingtons.

I climbed the slope with difficulty and walked back to the car. The clouds were darker overhead and the light was colourless, yet I felt warm. Perhaps the exercise had heated me. Or it may have been the glare that Mr McAlistair had sent in my direction when he turned and saw me watching him floundering in the mud, although I am fairly sure that I had managed to keep the smile off my face.

A few large flakes of snow were in the air by the time I reached the car, flakes so light and fluffy that they seemed to hang almost motionless. The wind had suddenly stilled and there was a hush in the air. I had intended to look for Allan Brindle and Mr Youngson, but within a minute the snow was falling as though determined to make up for a black Christmas. Within minutes, the scene was seasonable, pretty and worrying. If the snow kept up, the roads would soon be dangerous and the estate roads impassable without four-wheel drive. It was a scene to be enjoyed from behind double glazing and in front of a fire, drink in hand.

I decided to head for the office and write reports while the weather did its worst with the evidence. If Ian Kerr was still unaccounted for in the spring I would start looking for him again.

The tarmac roads were already slick. The steering felt disconcertingly light. It was as well that I kept my speed down, because after a mile or two a sudden white-out cut off all view of the outside world. I changed down and braked very lightly, slithering a little and waiting for the crunch, but came to a halt without hitting anything. The wipers began to cope again but the view through the windscreen was of a uniform whiteness. I crawled gently forward, assuring myself that there were no cliffs hereabouts and hoping for a clue as to where the verges of the road might be.

Dark shapes smudged faintly. I seemed to be safe for another yard or two. There was a gateway ahead and a small sign. I eased closer. The snow hesitated for a moment and I could read, 'Tundle House'.

Along the road I might meet another driver, equally disoriented, coming the other way. The driveway to Tundle House seemed to be sheltered by tall conifers. If I had to wait it out, I might as well do it in the company of a possibly useful witness. I pulled very gently into the driveway and crawled towards where I supposed the house must be. This soon took shape beyond a white expanse which I took to be gravel – a well-proportioned, two-storey house with crow-stepped gables. It was the middle of the day but lights were showing bright.

I got out of the car and ran and skidded to the front door. A porch kept the snow off me while I waited.

The bell was answered by an unimpressive young man in corduroys and an old sweater. 'You're parked on the lawn,' he said, 'but never mind for the moment. You'd better come inside. If you're selling something, you'll be out again in a moment, but we won't stand and argue with the door open.'

He led me through a hallway and into a living room where a log fire burned, supplementing the central heating. A huge, yellow Labrador, sprawled across the hearth-rug, glanced at us disinterestedly but soon resumed a rhythmic snoring. The house and its furnishings were old-fashioned, well kept and had what I can only call a grannyish charm. Some hi-fi equipment on a corner table looked almost outlandish.

'Did you want to phone for help?' the young man asked.

'I was looking for Andrew Nairn.'

'You've found him. What can I do for you?'

'You're Andy Nairn?' I said stupidly.

He sighed. 'Do I have to put on the gear and make-up and grease my hair? And, by the way, I don't give interviews.'

I had only seen him once or twice on television, and that by accident. He looked, of course, smaller in real life and his voice was educated, not the brash mid-Atlantic accent of show business. The whole image was different, but when I studied his features in isolation I could make out the wide-set eyes, the prominent cheekbones and above all the distinctive mouth which had hammered the music at an enraptured audience.

I identified myself and explained my visit.

'You'd better give me your coat and sit down,' he said. 'It seems that I do give interviews after all.'

He hung my coat over a chair beside a radiator and sat down opposite me in a wing-chair covered

90

with a printed material featuring a pattern of flowers and some improbable tropical birds.

'You're not my idea of a rock singer,' I told him.

He made a face. He must have been told the same a thousand times. 'I didn't set out to be that. It just happens to be the only thing I do well. I'd heard about the farmer disappearing,' he said. 'There was something about it on the radio. I was wondering whether I should come to you before I do my own disappearing act – I go off on a European tour in a couple of days. But I don't know that I can help.'

'Probably not,' I said. 'No more do I. Let's find out, shall we?'

He grinned, nodding.

The door bumped open and an elderly lady came in with a tray. Andrew Nairn was less than thirty, so I guessed that he had been a late baby – his mother must have been drawing the pension. The room came into focus. It had seemed outrageously inappropriate for a rock singer but it was the perfect setting for her faded prettiness.

'Andy had breakfast not long ago,' she said. 'He's a marvellous sleeper when he's on holiday. But I knew he'd be ready for coffee. And sensible people are having lunch about now. I was just making a sandwich for myself so I've added one for you. What a day you've chosen for a visit!'

She nodded and smiled and left the room without waiting for an introduction.

'My mum,' said the singer unnecessarily.

I re-seated myself. My day had started early and I was hungry. I could not identify all the components of the sandwich, but I recognised pâté, tomato and hardboiled egg between two rounds of toast. The coffee smelled superb.

'When you marry and leave home,' I said, 'can I adopt her?'

'Not a chance,' he said, grinning again. 'But I'll tell her you asked.'

My one desire was to get to grips with the sandwich without having to speak. 'Tell me about the pigeon-shoot,' I said.

'Right.' He settled down into the cushions of the chair while he thought about it. 'Landig Plant Hire were doing some work for me here – digging tracks for new drains, the old ones were clapped out and full of tree-roots. Steve McAlistair mentioned the pigeon-shoot to me.'

'He's a friend of yours?' I asked.

'A business acquaintance,' he said. I gathered that he had no more liking for Mr McAlistair than I had. 'I'd missed most of last season, although I managed to get a little quail-hunting in the States, so I said that I'd like to go along for both days. We were on Nuttleigh's for the first day but I was pleased when Steven told me that we were moving on to McKimber – I'm away so much that I can't shoot on a regular basis, but I've been grabbing the occasional day there whenever Jeffries had room for an extra Gun at driven birds or for the ducks. I've come to like those woods.

'I turned up early and the keeper put me where the ride leaves the estate road – you know the one I mean?'

I nodded. My mouth was full.

'I was getting some sport but not a lot. I could hear a lot of shooting around me and I guessed that the Guns at the fringes of the woods were turning the birds back. But the laird was at the other end of the ride and he packed it in early, came past me muttering something about brass monkeys. So I moved up to the edge of the wood where he'd been. I was in time to catch the best of it late on, when the birds had made up their minds that they were going to roost somewhere, come hell or high water.'

Hastily, I swallowed the last of the sandwich and washed it down with coffee. 'What time did you move up?' I asked.

'No idea. Going on for dusk.' He got up to put another log on the fire. 'If it's any help,' he said, 'a Land-Rover was leaving the wood where I'd been placed the week before and going back over the fields towards the farm.'

'Go on,' I said. 'You're coming to the vital period. You were overlooking the little wood?'

'That's right. That's where the farmer vanished from, isn't it? There was one more shot from there after I arrived. I could see the flash illuminating the treetops but I couldn't see a bird fall.

'I stayed quite late. My night vision's good and there was enough light in the sky to silhouette the birds. Somebody else was banging away to the north of me. I stayed for about an hour and then decided to jack it in. We'd picked up more than forty pigeon—'

'We?' I said quickly.

'Bess, my old Lab, and me,' he said. The Labrador bitch had woken again and she thumped her tail. 'We walked home after that. If it helps to fix the time, I could see what I took to be the same Land-Rover coming back down the fields.'

I tried not to frown. He had covered most of what I took to be the salient period, but without telling me what I wanted to hear. 'You didn't see or hear anybody moving around?'

'Not a damn thing – and, as I told you, my night vision's pretty good. And Bess always warns me if

93

somebody's moving nearby.' He stopped and thought, nursing his coffee. 'What's more,' he said suddenly, 'if anybody had come in my direction I'd have heard them. When you're shooting in near darkness you listen as much as you watch. I was near enough to the fence to hear it twang if somebody had climbed it; and frozen beech leaves make a hell of a noise as you walk through them.'

I led him through his story again without learning any more.

While we were speaking, the snowfall had almost stopped, although from the look of the sky there was more to come. My car was little more than a hump in the featureless white, but Andrew Nairn lent me a spade and a scraper and in about a quarter of an hour, wet and chilled through, I had the engine running and the windscreen clear and was back on the drive. Andrew Nairn had wanted to lend me a change of clothing, but in every direction he was several inches smaller than I was and I was damned if I was going to be a laughing-stock at Headquarters. The roads were treacherous but, taking it easy and refusing to come to a halt for anybody or anything, I made it back to Newton Lauder.

There was not much left of the working day. Rather than go home to change, I settled down in my small office, removed my wet shoes and sat on the radiator with my feet tucked up against its heat while I dictated a fresh report into a tape recorder. My report would later be typed up by a blind pool typist who usually managed to produce pages of beautiful typescript from my sometimes garbled ramblings, although now and again she would start off one key to the left or right of where she intended and produce a paragraph of gobbledegook.

I was replaying the tape and wondering whether I would be more likely to bring down the wrath of

94

the unpredictable Superintendent McHarg on my head if I did or did not add a few lines of speculation to the factual report when Mr Munro wandered in on one of his occasional aimless prowls through the building. I got up off the radiator.

'Sit down, sit down,' he said kindly, folding his skinny body, which always seemed to me to be a lashup of sticks and string, into the visitor's chair. It seemed to be one of his days for being a father-figure. He looked disapprovingly at the partially draped lady on my wall calendar and then averted his eyes. 'I suppose the man Kerr has not yet come back from whatever excesses he's been committing?'

My position on the radiator would have seemed an uneasy compromise between informality and remaining standing before a superior. Reluctantly, I went back to my cold chair. My feet immediately froze again.

'There's no sign of him,' I said. 'And no explanation for how he managed to disappear.'

Mr Munro was not interested in the absence of Ian Kerr, who he could picture in his disapproving, Calvinistic mind making whoopee with loose women and booze in whatever vision of a low dive such minds conjure up. 'This has been longer than his usual run of absences but I still think that he'll turn up,' he said. 'Have you made any more progress with this poaching affair?'

I produced the annotated list of potential suspects. He was interested, but he drew in a sharp breath when he saw some of the names and his long face took on the expression of one who has found, after putting on his slippers, that the cat had messed in one of them. 'Out of the question,' he said. He snatched a pencil off my desk and ran it through several names. 'A magistrate, a regional councillor and my own doctor,' he said. 'What are you thinking of?'

95

All three vocations had in the past produced expo-
nents of more serious crimes than poaching but I decided
not to argue the point. 'I'm not thinking anything,' I said
feebly. 'This isn't a list of suspects, it's a comprehensive
list of people who know the ground well . . . for elimi-
nation purposes.'

'Then eliminate these gentlemen—'

He was interrupted by the telephone. Superintendent
McHarg came on the line. He wished, he said, to discuss
my last report.

'Things have moved on since that was written,' I
said. 'I've just dictated another report. Shall I give
you the gist of it or will you wait until you get the fax
copy?'

'Play the tape to me over the phone.'

'Mr Munro's with me, sir,' I said.

'Let the old fool hear it too.'

'I heard that,' the Chief Superintendent said hotly.
'He—'

'And I heard him,' Mr McHarg said. If there was any
apology in his tone, the telephone failed to transmit it.
'Play the tape.'

I made an apologetic face at Mr Munro, plugged a lead
into the tape recorder, attached a rubber sucker to the
phone and started the tape. Chief Superintendent Munro
listened intently to my taped voice. Superintendent
McHarg must have done the same although he was
strangely silent when the taped report had finished –
wondering, I had no doubt, whether to castigate me for
crying wolf or to enquire why I was sitting on my arse
– his usual expression – instead of dashing about in the
snow, doing something clever.

'I thought we had agreed,' Munro said loudly – I
held out the instrument, to make sure that Mr McHarg
could catch his words – 'that Mr Kerr would return of

his own accord in the fullness of time and that you would concentrate your efforts on the poaching incidents at McKimber Estate.'

'There's a possibility,' I said, 'that the two cases are connected.'

Mr Munro might be old, as policemen go, but he was far from being the old fool Mr McHarg had called him. 'You think that Mr Kerr may have entered McKimber grounds in pursuit of what I believe they call a "runner" and have disturbed the poacher at work? But the keeper states that he was not visited that night.'

'He did hear an engine. The poacher may have been interrupted before he could begin work,' I said. 'Or there's the possibility that Mr Kerr himself was the poacher—'

'Stuff and nonsense!' Munro exploded.

That was quite sufficient to make up Mr McHarg's mind for him. 'Sergeant,' he said sharply.

'Sir?'

'You may have something there. Or you may not. There are gaps in the evidence. Not your fault,' he added with uncharacteristic generosity. 'Between the contractor's operations and the weather, what evidence there might have been is buried. Then again, the period between your leaving the scene and your return is barely accounted for. It would only take one witness – any one witness – to be mistaken or lying to make a gap that Kerr could very easily have slipped through.' (Mr Munro grunted agreement.) 'At this stage, if we were to fetch the digger driver back from Spain or start digging up the water main, we'd have our balls in a sling if Kerr did return, hungover but otherwise unharmed. I don't think that he will, but he might. In view of the weather . . . we'll wait. Continue with your enquiries. I've a good mind to send you some help.'

'The road over Soutra is blocked,' Munro said with satisfaction.

McHarg pretended not to have heard him. 'If the digger driver – Campbell, is it? – fails to return on his due date, we might make a bid for extradition. But,' he added quickly, 'if somebody has to fly out to Spain, don't go getting any ideas that it'll be you. And when the thaw comes, we can bring in the thermal imaging cameras and sniffer dogs. Until then, carry on. If Mr Munro won't sign your mileage claim, bring it to me. And keep me posted. You understand?'

'Of course, sir,' I said. 'It might be useful to have all mobiles keep an eye open for Hempie Wright.'

'I'll fix that. What's the number of his van?'

'I don't know. Swansea couldn't tell me. If you know the number they can tell you the owner's name but not the other way around.'

I heard him snort. 'You're about as much use as a crick in the neck,' he said.

'Before you hang up,' Mr Munro said, 'I will speak to the Superintendent.' He looked at his watch. 'Your shift is almost over. Go home and change your wet clothes before you catch your death of cold. I appreciate your zeal but would prefer that you tempered it with a little common sense.'

I gave him the phone, grabbed up my shoes and cleared out in a hurry. When superiors fall out, the wise man climbs a tree and pulls it up after him.

FIVE

Like any other citizen, a policeman needs to protect his modest savings against inflation if he is to know comfort in later life. The best investment is to buy a home. Here, the rootless nature of the job and the rules of service put the copper at a disadvantage; but obstacles are for surmounting and I had been lucky. Edinburgh property values had boomed and I had sold my Old Town tenement flat for substantially more than the amount of my mortgage. This had enabled me, with the aid of the building society and the approval of Mr Munro in one of his rare moods of bonhomie, to buy a small but comfortable flat in the better part of Newton Lauder.

We had an evening date. Deborah had let herself into the flat, bringing several of the pigeons which we had gathered at the big shoot, a favourite recipe of her mother's and a bottle of Keith's wine.

It was snowing again as I reached home, but Deborah had lit the logs in the grate and the flat was warm and welcoming. From the kitchen came a smell that nearly had me dribbling down my chin. The hot bath and change into dry clothes, to which I had been looking forward, seemed irrelevant but I took them anyway.

I had never realised that the humble woodpigeon

could be such a delicacy. We dined well on pigeon pie, washed up and settled on the couch to watch a film on the box.

The film wound itself up to a predictably emotional finish. I got up, turned off the set, started a longplaying tape of assorted music and made coffee.

We talked. Inevitably our talk turned towards the two mysteries at McKimber. I would not usually discuss police business with an outsider, but Deborah and her family can be very discreet when discretion is called for and her knowledge of local affairs and personalities exceeds even that of her father.

I was still carrying Allan Brindle's list, by now heavily annotated, creased and crumpled. Deborah smoothed it out on her knee. 'Let's see the list of dates when McKimber was poached,' she said. I produced it. 'I thought so.' She put her finger on a name. 'This lad was working on an oil-rig all winter. Two weeks on and two off. His dates couldn't possibly fit. And Johnny Bates came ratting with me last month. He brought his only airgun and it was a one-seven-seven. And look here . . .'

Mr Youngson and Chief Superintendent Munro had cast doubt on most of the more respectable names on the list. Now Deborah began to eliminate many of the beaters. It said a lot about her life-style that she knew so much intimate history about most of the rougher characters in and around Newton Lauder. When she had exhausted her local knowledge she looked the list over again with a critical eye.

'Eleven possibles,' she said, 'including six probables. And by far the most likely name is Hempie Wright – not as the main character, his feet are too small, but as the occasional companion.'

'And nobody seems to have set eyes on him since

Saturday night,' I said. 'I suppose that he and Ian Kerr wouldn't have gone off to raise hell together?'

'Un-uh. They didn't get on. Ian caught Hempie nicking from his barn and gave him a leathering. I'd rather believe that Hempie had . . . disposed of Mr Kerr and made himself scarce. I don't believe it, but I could believe it easier than the other thing.' She gave me back my lists. 'Tell me about Andy Nairn,' she said.

'He can't be the poacher,' I said. 'He's away too much.'

'Of course not, you ass! But it's interesting to know what somebody's really like when you've only seen him performing. On stage, he comes over as larger than life. Terribly macho and sort of dangerous. You could imagine him leading a motorcycle gang, terrorising a small town and raping innocent maidens like me. Could we give him an invitation when he gets back from his tour?'

'To dinner, you mean?'

'I hadn't thought of dinner,' she said in a thoughtful tone. 'I was thinking more of rabbiting, or a day at the clay pigeons.' Deborah's idea of a social occasion differs from that of most of her sex.

'You'd be disappointed,' I told her. 'Rape would come very low on the agenda. He comes over as a well-mannered laddie who enjoys a quiet life in the country. He was studying piano, he told me. His father had a financial setback, so he joined up with a few friends who'd formed a spare-time group to make a little money on the side and they caught on. The rest seemed to happen of its own accord. It hasn't gone to his head. He doesn't take himself seriously, though he's deadly serious about his singing.'

'And he gave up the piano?' Deborah said sadly. She was picturing a concert pianist lost to the world.

'He doesn't mind that. He doesn't think he'd ever

have made the top rank. He says that it's a relief, not having to protect his hands all the time.'

The fire was burning badly. I got up to rearrange the logs. When I was seated again, she turned and leaned back against me, pulling my arm around her shoulders. 'He may be a country chiel,' she said, 'but he's wrong about one thing. I bet I could have walked through McKimber woods without making a sound. The wind would have swept the beech leaves into piles, leaving most of the ground bare.'

'Maybe. But he was waiting, on a quiet night, listening for the sound of birds' wings. Would he have missed the sound of somebody getting over or under or through the fence? You know how sound travels along the wires, especially the squeak as the wire's pulled through a staple.'

'If I wanted to pass the fence quietly, I'd roll under the bottom wire.'

'But that supposes that you wanted to sneak through,' I pointed out. 'Ian Kerr had no reason to do that. Even if he was running off with a woman or going on a skite, it wouldn't have made any difference if he'd shaken hands with every Gun on McKimber.' It was looking less and less likely to me that Ian Kerr had gone off of his own accord. 'And I bet you couldn't manoeuvre a dead body past the fence without making it twang like a harp. Why didn't you mention the handicapped son?' I asked.

'I'd forgotten all about him,' she said. 'Or, to be truthful, I suppose I'd pushed him to the back of my mind. I haven't seen him for years. They keep him quietly at home and never mention him. It's become a local convention to avoid the subject. Nobody ever asks after him. The Kerrs seem to prefer it that way.'

'Is he violent?'

I felt her laugh silently. 'No. Just a bit dottled.'

'And his father? You've known Mr Kerr longer than I have. I've only met him twice for a few minutes each time. Would he be the type to commit suicide?'

'I'd think not,' she said slowly. 'When things got too much for him, he'd get it out of his system by having a flaming row with somebody, or going on the bash, or . . .' She stopped dead.

'I know about the other woman,' I said. 'Or women.'

'Oh. Well that doesn't seem to make him the sort of person who'd kill himself. Does it?'

'I suppose not.'

We fell silent, thinking.

Our relationship had been an unusual one for a permissive age. We had developed a deep friendship which was delicately balanced between passionate and platonic. Each of us was aware of the other's sexuality. But Deborah was physically shy, forthcoming with minor caresses but wary of any deeper intimacy. I thought that she was a virgin rather than that she had suffered in an affair, and later I learned that I was right.

Shortly before I met Deborah, I had ended an affair with a lady solicitor who had been so sexually voracious that for a time sex had become no more than a tedious chore. I was in no hurry to re-activate that side of my life. I was content to wait. Some day the time would be right and sex, this time with love, would once again be as marvellous as it had been when I was young and the world of love was new. Deborah, putting a different interpretation on my restraint, seemed to feel both grateful and, at times, slighted.

As we talked, and perhaps because our minds were far away, these inhibitions had faded into the distant background. Our bodies may have been doing our thinking. A caress had become a fondle, a peck on the cheek became a fullblooded kiss. My hand, which had been holding hers, had found a happier resting place. I realised suddenly that we were both short of breath. Her eyes, which had been reflecting the firelight, were now closed; and if she had moved her elbow an inch she would have discovered that my body was almost painfully aware of hers.

I pressed gently on her shoulder and she came round as if I had hauled her. We were in a kiss which I thought and prayed would never end. The touch of lip and tongue was magical as never before, an irresistible incitement to explore more deeply. I felt a surge of joy. The moment was right at last. If it were to happen now, by mutual desire, it would be the ultimate perfection and we would enter a new age of wonder.

The telephone blew the moment to hell and further. My erection subsided. Deborah, very pink about the ears, smoothed down her skirt and moved away from me.

I picked up the phone. A woman's voice said, 'Sergeant Fellowes?'

So it was police business.

'This is Mrs Brindle. Allan just spoke to me on the radio. He said to tell you that the poacher's here.'

'I'll come straight away,' I said.

As it turned out, that promise erred on the optimistic side. I would have set off immediately, but Deborah first insisted that I clad myself suitably – which, in her view, meant sweaters, wellingtons and my old oilskin coat complete with hood – and then decided that she was coming with me.

Several minutes were wasted in futile (on my part) argument before she added what proved to be the clincher. 'If it's still snowing,' she said, 'you'll get stuck in your own car. But I've got Dad's jeep.'

'Give me the keys.'

'It's not insured for you,' she said. 'If you prang it you pay for it.'

I gave in, not very gracefully.

We left the flat together after another delay while she put a guard on the fire and switched off the percolator. The snow had stopped again, but recently. The moon was up in a clearing sky. While Deborah swept her arm over the jeep's windscreen, I grabbed my police radio and the McKimber walkie-talkie out of my car. Then we were away.

While Deborah drove – carefully and in four-wheel drive – I first used my personal radio to report my journey to Control. 'Is there a car in the vicinity of McKimber Estate?' I asked.

'There's a car returning from the site of a road accident near Dryburgh,' Control told me. 'They could be at McKimber in fifteen or twenty minutes.'

'Ask them to circle the estate, looking for wheel tracks, and then to stand by in case I need help,' I said. 'I'm on my way to a poaching incident.'

I fumbled in layers of clothing to pocket the radio. Then I switched to the other one. Its controls were unfamiliar and I wasted some time talking to myself and listening to nothing before I managed to make contact with the keeper.

'Mr Brindle? Over.'

'Where are you, Sergeant? Over.' His voice was muted, as though he was speaking softly and very close to the microphone to avoid alerting his quarry.

'Approaching McKimber, arriving . . .' I looked out at a changed landscape but was lucky enough to recognise the gates of Tundle House. 'In about five minutes. Over.'

'There's two of them and I think I've got the buggers

105

cornered,' Brindle said. 'Park at position B and move quietly to . . . Got the map there? Over.'

The map was in one of my pockets. 'Got it. Over.'

'Come to the K in McKimber. I'll be near the letter R. Over and out.'

With some difficulty I got out the map and tried to read it by the faint illumination from the dash. Fortunately I had already studied it with care. Rendezvous B was at the back of the big house. The name of the estate was spread over its acres. It seemed that Brindle had pinned down his quarry in a large peninsula of woodland which jutted into an area of level fields. Anyone trying to escape through the fields would cast a long shadow across the snow.

'Up the main drive,' I told Deborah, 'and round the back of the house.'

'You've got it,' she said.

'Go down to sidelights as soon as you're in at the gates.'

The snow in the driveway was unblemished by wheel tracks, but Deborah held the middle between bushes which sprang black out of nothingness. The house reared up in front of us. She coaxed the jeep round to the back, crawling as quietly as the small vehicle could manage, and parked beside some outbuildings. Around the house was a tangled web of footprints. Some faint grooves suggested wheel tracks which had been made between the two falls of snow.

'You wait here,' I said. 'Lock yourself in.'

'Hold on. I'm coming—'

'No you are not. This could get rough.'

'All the more reason—'

For once, I was more determined than she was. 'Promise, or I'll handcuff you to the steering wheel.'

She probably guessed that I had no handcuffs with

me, but she could see that I was adamant. 'All right,' she said. 'All bloody *right!*'

I closed the door gently and set off. I walked as quietly as I could and although the fresh snow squeaked underfoot it also seemed to muffle sound.

I followed the estate road to the first curve. Every tree could have hidden a hostile presence. The poachers were only known to have used an airgun, but that was not to say that they did not have shotguns with them.

The map had shown a succession of clearings leading off to the left; and a gap in the trees seemed to lead in the right direction. I turned off, floundered through deeper snow and joined up with another set of footprints, clearly marked by the bright moonlight.

'Where are you?' demanded the radio in my pocket softly. 'Over.'

I fished it out. 'Following a set of footprints along the clearings towards Letter K. Yours? Over.'

'Aye. Keep coming. Out.'

I kept coming. The line of clearings had seemed clearcut on the map, but there had been some planting and some felling since the map was drawn and the tracery of the trees, sometimes confused by snow lying on the branches, was less distinct. I decided to follow the footprints.

After a hundred yards another set of human footprints and those of a small dog joined up with the first set. Did Allan Brindle have a companion? Then I realised that he had come across a set of the poacher's tracks and followed them. Further on another set converged and the three seemed to proceed together. Into my mind came the story by A. A. Milne in which Pooh Bear walks round and round a small wood, following an ever increasing number of his own tracks. Surely I couldn't have walked in a circle? In these damned, confusing woods, anything was possible. But no, because one set swung away again.

Ahead I could see a broad splash of moonlight marking another and larger clearing. Two sets of prints and those of the dog departed to my right. I decided that the poachers had parted and that Brindle had decided to follow one of them. The other set went left and I went after it.

I had trudged perhaps a third of the way around the open space when the footprints before me were again joined. This time it seemed that somebody had come down from the branches of a large tree to join the other. Were there three poachers then? Or had Brindle's quarry evaded him, hidden in a tree and then joined up with his mate? I hurried on, puzzling. Both sets of footprints were small. There had been no marks to show how he had first arrived at the tree. Surely he could not have waited aloft since the snowfall began?

I stood still and thought about it. He or they must know that clearcut tracks were being left in the snow. In such circumstances, what would I have done?

Then it hit me. I turned and galumphed back as swiftly as I could through the hampering snow. In his boots, I would have walked on until I reached the ground under a clump of conifers, or some other place where footprints would not show. Then I would have returned, walking backwards, to a climbable tree and waited for pursuit to go past . . .

That was what he had done. He was already at the foot of the large tree, a small figure barely distinguishable in what seemed to be white clothing. He had started to walk off, again in reverse, but when I came into view he turned and began to run. I was relieved to see that there was no sign of a gun.

He was between me and the large clearing. Rather

108

than cross the open he set off around the perimeter, giving me a chance to cut the corner.

Contours were impossible to judge beneath the snow. He seemed to be at a lower level than I was, but when I launched my tackle the bank took me by surprise. I arrived in his path much sooner and travelling very much faster than I had intended – indeed, I would have shot past in front of him if I had not flung out a hand, in the hope more of arresting myself than him, and by a fluke caught and held a handful of clothing.

The jerk swung us both off our feet. He had time to utter one very rude word in broad Scots before we fell together. There was a gut-watering groan of ice and I realised that the expanse of snow overlaid a frozen duck-pond. A flighting pond, Deborah called it later.

We slid, pushing up pillows of snow before us. Powdery snow was forced up my sleeves and down my neck, into my eyes and hair. The tops of my boots scooped up a load of it.

Later, I realised that we had been skidding towards the corner where the feeder stream had kept the water open. If we had reached it, we would have been in for a ducking in freezing water if nothing worse. But our mad slither brought us to a place where the tips of reeds or waterweed had been showing on the surface. It was as if I had tried to sledge on a gravel drive without, of course, the sledge. I slowed so suddenly that my captive rolled on top of me.

We came to a halt. He rolled off my head and I sat up. He remained face down, catching his breath. He seemed to be wearing a set of loose painter's overalls over his ordinary clothes. I still had hold of one of his sleeves.

'Hempie Wright, I presume,' I said.

'That,' he said, 'depends.'

'Depends on what?'

Instead of answering, he began to struggle, flailing around like a mad thing. I was uncomfortably aware that ice tends to be thin where reeds reach the surface but I was damned if I was letting go. I thought that he had meant to say that it depended on whether he could break out of my grip. But, if that were the case, why was he yelling his head off?

Movement caught my eye, a black figure at the edge of the pond. Was Wright yelling to his companion for armed help? But then I recognised the sturdy figure and the thumbstick of Allan Brindle.

'Calm down,' I told Wright. 'It's over. You're nicked.'

He rolled over and sat up suddenly, producing an ominous creak from the ice. Even by moonlight I could see that his face was as pale as his overalls. He seemed to be gibbering, too overcome to speak, but he was pointing downwards.

'You've broken a leg?' I said.

He shook his head violently and pointed again.

Our slide across a corner of the pond had swept away the snow and left a long streak of darker ice. Where Wright had been lying, his body had melted the surface, forming a more transparent patch, as if a hand had been wiped across a misted windscreen.

Beneath the ice but close to it, a pattern of light and darkness showed. I tried to convince myself that it was anything but what I knew it to be. When a companion points out an image in the clouds or in the embers of a fire, it may be impossible at first to see it. But once seen, it is inescapable. The shadows under the ice had formed themselves into a face and they refused to revert to a mere pattern of pond-weed and debris. It stared up at me, tilted roguishly, and it smiled with a grin that sent a primeval dread crawling from my fundament, up my spine and into my scalp.

I made an effort and regained some control of my voice. 'If I let go of you, you won't try and run for it?' I said to Wright.

'My knees've gone to water,' he whispered.

'Don't shake your head,' I said urgently. 'This ice is thin. Stay a few yards behind me and crawl very gently towards Mr Brindle.'

But he made the mistake of looking down again. His nerve broke. He tore his sleeve out of my grasp, jumped to his feet and ran for the bank. Like some cartoon character, he seemed to skim over the surface by dint of sheer speed; but I heard and felt the ice crack.

After testing the ice for himself, Brindle had wisely decided to remain on the bank. He pounced on Hempie Wright and shook him. 'You're no' the one I'm after,' he said. 'Where's your mate?'

'Hold on a moment,' I said. 'There seems to be a body under the ice. I'll join you if I can.'

I had a choice between crossing the width of the pond over an uncertain depth of water or following where Hempie Wright had gone before. I chose the shorter course as being presumably shallower. I tried to make myself light and to walk very gently, but I was only halfway to the bank before the ice gave way and I went through. The water only came to my knees. From there on, I had to wade, breaking the ice as I went. I nearly repeated Mr McAlistair's trick of walking out of my boots, but by curling up my toes I made it to the bank with my footwear complete.

'Is't Ian Kerr?' Brindle asked quickly.

I lay down and lifted my legs to empty my boots. Half the water seemed to run up inside my trousers. 'Impossible to say for sure, but I'd bet money on it. Well, he isn't going anywhere—'

We were interrupted by the arrival of a large Labrador which I would have mistaken for Sam except that he tried very hard to lick my face. Sam had never paid me more than the scantest attention.

He turned out to be Sam after all. As I got to my feet, Deborah came flying out of the trees and threw herself at me. 'Are you all right?' she asked, over and over again.

'Of course I'm all right,' I said testily.

'But your face . . .'

I realised that my face was stinging. 'What's wrong with it?' I asked.

'It's all blood.'

I remembered that my face had taken the brunt of my contact with the roughened ice. 'Just scratches,' I said. 'I thought I told you to stay in the car.'

'Yes, but I had to come and tell you. You'll never guess what I saw.'

'I can guess exactly what you saw,' I told her. 'You'll never guess – oh, never mind! There's a body under the ice.'

'Ian Kerr?'

'Impossible to say, but it seems likely.' I shrugged off a sense of *déjà vu* and felt in my pockets. I seemed to have parted company with my police radio along the way and when I took hold of the McKimber one several bits came away in my fingers. 'Call your wife up,' I told Brindle. 'Ask her to phone the police and tell them that we've found a body. There's a car somewhere in this area. They're to meet you at your cottage and one of you bring them back here. Newton Lauder can report to Edinburgh and then start the routine for a suspicious death. I'll join you shortly but there's something I must do first.'

'Can I come with you?' Deborah asked. The fact

112

that she asked instead of insisting was a step in the right direction.

'Better not,' I said. 'I'll be with you in minutes. There's no danger now.' Except, I thought, that if the shape under the ice turned out to be a plastic bag I'd be in the running for being voted Prat of the Year by the Lothian and Borders Constabulary.

I set off through the snow at a clumsy jog-trot, squelching at every step. I deviated slightly from the shortest route in order to pass the scene of my flying tackle. A rectangular hole in the snow, out on the ice, marked the fall of my radio. I did not fancy another trip on to ice which was almost certainly cracked, but it was that or pay for the radio. I shuffled gently out and retrieved it. It was unbroken but there seemed to be no point in using it. The routine for dealing with a fatality would already be in train and the question of tyre-marks in the roads around the estate had become academic. I flipped up my hood before realising that it was full of snow and jogged on towards the big house.

No lights were showing, but this neither surprised nor deterred me. I hammered on the big front door and rang the bell and, after a long interval, lights came on and shuffling footsteps approached.

The door was opened by the laird himself. Mr Youngson was in slippers, pyjamas and a dressing-gown. His hair was tousled and he yawned, giving a good impression of a man newly awakened from a deep sleep.

'What on earth do you want, Sergeant, at this ungodly hour?'

'I need to talk to you, urgently,' I said.

'What about?'

'I've just discovered a dead body in your grounds.' To avoid repetition of the question that Deborah and

113

Allan Brindle had asked, I added, 'It may or may not be Ian Kerr.'

He blinked at me and then reluctantly stood aside. 'You'd better come in,' he said.

That was all I needed. He had invited me inside. I pushed past him and headed for the back of the house. He followed me, protesting loudly, but I ignored him. If I were wrong, he could have me hauled over the coals; but for once I felt sure of my ground.

I found what I was looking for in a small cloak-room – a set of painter's overalls, soaking wet, had been thrown down beside the door to a lavatory; in a basket was a cairn terrier, also wet; and an air rifle stood in a corner beside the corpse of a cock pheasant.

The house managed to seem even colder than the outdoors and my teeth were beginning to chatter, but I managed to speak with reasonable clarity. 'I thought as much,' I said. 'You slipped past us back to the house. It never occurred to us to put your name on the list. But when I realised that anybody who didn't have one of the estate radios and familiarity with the estate map would be almost certain to leave tracks where Brindle or I would cross them, I thought of you immediately. And Deborah Calder was sitting in a car at the back of the house. She saw you go by.'

'I don't know what you're talking about,' he said. The anger in his voice had turned to defiance.

'Hempie Wright found the body,' I told him. 'It scared him out of his wits. I should think that he's babbled the whole story to Allan Brindle by now.'

He stood still for a long moment. Then he gave a sudden shiver. 'That would certainly give him the shock of his life,' he said. 'Did he do that to your face? If so, it was in panic. There's no vice in him. But you realise that a man in that state would say whatever he thought his interrogator wanted to hear?'

'And sign it,' I said.

He lifted and dropped his hands in a helpless gesture. 'Come into the kitchen. It's the only warm place in the house, but Mrs Mac gets upset if I hang around there during the day.'

He led the way into a large kitchen, more modern than the rest of the house but featuring a solid fuel range. The warmth from this was suddenly the most welcoming sensation in the world. We stood as close to it as we could without actually scorching.

'I don't admit a damn thing,' he said. 'So what do you think you're going to do about it.'

'How did Ian Kerr's body arrive in your duck-pond?' I asked him.

'I honest-to-God do not have the faintest idea. Nor, I'm as certain as one can be, does Hempie. What I told you the first time you came was the absolute truth. Have you considered suicide?'

'We don't know yet how he died,' I said. 'When we do, we'll know whether accident and suicide are possibilities. But, on what we know at the moment, it seems most likely that he was murdered. If that proves to be the case, the supposition is bound to arise that he left his shooting position to gather a bird, saw something that incriminated the two poachers and was killed to shut his mouth.'

'But it didn't happen,' he said, as if that would settle the matter.

'Perhaps not. But do you think the police and a subsequent court would be more likely to believe you if the poaching matter had been cleared up, or if you were protesting your innocence of both crimes while the evidence that you were poaching is damning?'

He thought that over in silence. I could tell that he did not like it at all. 'You keep talking about a crime,' he said plaintively at last. 'But you're forgetting that it's my land.'

'I'm not forgetting it. But you leased the sporting rights. What would you call a man who sold something and then stole it back?'

'A bird released into the wild doesn't belong to anybody,' he said. 'When it's dead it becomes the property of the man who killed it.'

'Not if it's stolen out of a catching pen,' I pointed out. 'Technically, what you say is true. But morally? Your counsel may be able to argue that a landowner can't poach off his own sporting tenant, but I wouldn't want to risk a murder charge on the strength of it. Hempie Wright is certainly vulnerable and you were acting together.'

He thought again and swore under his breath. 'I'm an old fool,' he said. 'I thought I'd driven a good bargain with Jeffries, but what he paid me for the use of the land was derisory. Peanuts! And he wants me to renew on the same terms! Do you know what that bastard charges his clients?' he asked. 'While I had to rely for my shooting on invitations from friends?'

It is often a mistake to get drawn into argument. But I liked the old man. I thought that he was probably innocent of anything worse than mischief, but his attitude was going to do him no good. 'I've no idea,' I said. 'But by the time he's leased the rights from you, reared the poults, paid Allan Brindle and his under-keeper for a year, hired beaters and met his advertising costs, it would have to be hefty.'

Another silence. 'I never thought of it that way,' he said sadly. 'Does this have to come out?'

'I'll have to make a report,' I said. 'With an unsolved

116

murder under investigation, it can't be hidden. But do you want my advice?'

'No,' he said quickly, and then, 'Yes. I think I do.'

'Get Jeffries on the phone now, right away. Never mind if you have to wake him up. Tell him that you've been a fool. Admit everything. Then offer to renew for several years at the same terms.'

'He'll nail me to the wall!'

'Cheap at the price if he agrees not to prosecute,' I told him. 'Remember what lawyers cost. And those invitations from friends will dry up if you're convicted of poaching.'

'That's true,' he said. 'I'll do it.' He studied my face for a long moment. 'You're a good sort,' he said. 'Go easy on Hempie. This was my folly. Envy and boredom. Hempie just came along now and again for the fun of it.'

'Easily led,' I suggested.

He made a face. *'Touché!'*

'Do it now,' I said. 'And then, don't go to bed. You'll have visitors.'

SIX

It was not far to Allan Brindle's house but in my wet state I was chilled through again by the time I reached its welcoming warmth. Any more hypothermia, I decided, and there would be another corpse in the case. Two other cars had found parking space around Brindle's Land-Rover.

In a living room largely decorated with mounted antlers and stuffed birds, I found Brindle and Hempie Wright seated in basket chairs on either side of a blazing fire, sharing the dregs of a bottle of whisky. They seemed to be on friendly terms. The keeper was evidently prepared to bury the hatchet once he was sure that the poaching would stop. Wright was calmer but his eyes were wary.

'Well?' Brindle said. 'Was it who we thought?'

'Wait and see,' I told him, as I peeled off the coat and sweaters which were keeping warmth out rather than in. I kicked off my boots and emptied the dregs into the coal-scuttle. 'Where's Miss Calder?'

'I could hardly leave this rogue by himself, so my wife went to show the two policemen the way. She's not back yet. So when the doctor turned up I told him he'd only have to follow a' the tracks in the snow. He said what if the moon went behind a cloud and his torch went out? So your lassie went to hold his

119

hand in a manner of speaking.' The last words came back to me through at least one doorway. Brindle returned and tossed me a pair of thick socks and a towel.

Of the local doctors who acted as police surgeons, only one was nervous and excessively cautious. 'Dr Lasswade?' I asked.

'That's just who it was.' Brindle picked up the empty bottle. 'I'm sorry, but this was the last of it. It was just the tail-end of one of the bottles Mr Jeffries supplies to keep the beaters warm. But there's tea in the pot or beer in the fridge.'

I finished towelling my hair and poured a mug of hot tea. The last thing I wanted was a bellyful of chilled beer. I sat down beside Wright. I was seeing him for the first time other than by moonlight. His small frame was topped by a head of ordinary size, so that it looked too large for his body. His hair was silver, as was the stubble on a face that had started out amiable and ordinary but had been given character by the effects of time and weather.

'Now,' I said. 'Tell me what you know about the body.'

He jumped so that the basket chair squeaked. 'Nothing,' he said. He gave a nervous look at the notebook on my knee. 'God, but it gave me a fright! That was the first I knew of it, other than that Mr Kerr was missing. But maybe it's not himself.'

'And maybe it is,' I said. 'Tell me about Saturday afternoon, up until the time you left McKimber.'

'I never left McKimber,' he said. 'The laird said I could bide. He said it was no weather for me to be living rough. I'm sleeping in the chauffeur's room above the garage and my van's inside. He made room for it, atween the Range Rover and the Jag.'

So the laird had lied to me about Wright's where-abouts. 'I thought that he was supposed to be broke,' I said.

'It's temporary,' said Brindle. 'Or so he hopes. He raised every penny he could to stake his son in business, but he kept the cars.'

That made sense. I looked at Wright. 'Tell me about the pigeon-shoot.'

'But nothing *happened*,' he said. 'The laird said I was to be allowed on the shoot and given a good place. I was fine pleased. The game dealer was paying as much for a pigeon as for a pheasant – crazy, the way prices are just now.'

'That's for sure,' said the keeper.

'Mr Brindle put me at the edge of the woods, looking over the boundary between Miscally and Nuttleigh's.'

'Time?'

'Noon, about. I kept back from the edge at first, to be hidden, but I never had the knack of shooting through branches. So I found myself a hidey-hole atween twa holly trees in the hedge, where I could see the birds coming and get a clear shot but they couldn't see me.'

'And you could see the countryside below?'

'Aye. I'd a grandstand view when something drew my eye. Whenever the cushies stopped moving, I'd go out and pick up my birds. I didno' look down often.'

'But when you did look down, what did you see?'

'I saw twa men settle in the strip of trees below me. Then a mannie and a lass came to the wee wood and put decoys out and she went back up to the bigger wood. He bided there, shooting, until another man, who I thought looked like Mr Kerr but I couldn't quite make him out, came from the direction of Nuttleigh's and sent him off. In atween, the farmer on Nuttleigh's came down in a vehicle and went back. He came twice more—'

121

'Twice?' I asked sharply.

'Aye. Just afore the sun went down and again later when it was dark. I could only see the headlights that time and the flashing of torches but it sounded like the same vehicle.'

I had forgotten about our search for Ian Kerr after the shoot, as far as we were concerned, was over. 'Go on,' I said.

'Nothing to go on about. There was another lad stayed shooting late, but he left when it was real dark. I waited, and when the moon came out the cushies were still unsettled and on the move. But Mr Brindle came after me, in a right rage, and told me the shoot was past and I was to bugger off.'

'I never—' Brindle began.

'He didn't say it quite like that, but that's what he meant. Well, it was fair enough. I made him wait while I picked up the last of my birds – I'd got sixty-three all told, for seventy-one cartridges. So I came back to the big house and the laird gied me a dram.'

'Who and what else did you see or hear?' I asked him.

'You want to know about foxes and owls?'

'Not particularly,' I said. 'Stick to humans.'

'Then not a damn soul. Even while it was dark it was still and so quiet you could have heard a flea fart. There was nobody else, after the other chiel went.'

The 'other chiel' would have been Andrew Nairn. 'If that's Ian Kerr's body in the pond,' I said, 'he got from the small wood on Nuttleigh's up to the pond on McKimber.'

'No' while I was there,' Wright said firmly. 'Or, if he did, he went a' the way round by the roads.'

I thought it over. Wright seemed to believe what he was saying. If there was a lie among his words it was a small boast; I decided that nobody, not even Deborah,

122

could kill sixty-three woodpigeon with only eight misses.

Allan Brindle was thinking the same. 'You were waiting until the birds were down,' he said.

"Course I was,' Wright agreed. Obviously, he felt that anyone who fired at a bird on the wing when he could wait for it to settle was wasting valuable cartridges.

Brindle caught my eye. 'Late on,' he said, 'the others had gone to their homes. Anyone could walk through the woods, even carrying a body on his back, without meeting a soul.' Hempie Wright began to protest. Brindle talked over the top of him. 'But,' he said, 'look at his boots.'

I looked. Wright was wearing heavy shooting boots of suede leather. I recognised the make. Keith had offered me a pair, but even at a discount they were too expensive for a working copper.

'The laird gied me these,' Hempie said proudly. 'They belonged to that son of his. Too small for himself they were, but they fit me fine.'

'That's by the by. Point is,' Brindle said, 'that anyone carrying a body to the pond and putting it where you found it would get his boots wet. I wear boots much like those myself. They keep the wet out fine – the only way water can get inside is over the top – but you can see they've been in water for hours after. When I went to chase this old rascal away at the end of the shoot, his boots were dry. I noticed while I was wondering to myself where he stole them.'

I imagined myself single-handedly carrying a body of no little weight to the feeder stream and pushing it under the ice. I had to admit that it would have been impossible without getting my feet wet. But had Hempie Wright necessarily been single-handed? I tried to formulate a trick question that would determine

123

whether the laird had been in the woods again that night.

But voices could be heard outside, then footsteps in the little hallway. The living room door opened and Deborah and Mrs Brindle ushered Dr Lasswade into the room. Their manner was deferential. In country districts, the doctor ranks with the minister. There was an interval of confusion while they removed coats and, in the doctor's case, galoshes. The three basket chairs were already in use. Brindle rose and gave his up to Deborah before helping his wife to bring more chairs from the kitchen.

I caught Deborah's eye. She looked shaken and so white that she was almost green, but she managed to nod. So the body was that of Ian Kerr. I had had little doubt of it.

The doctor accepted a mug of tea. 'What happened to your face?'

'I had a fall.'

'Damn nearly had one myself,' he said. 'It's slippery out there. I'll clean it up for you in a minute or two. Silly business, being fetched from my bed to confirm that the man was dead. As if he could possibly have had a spark of life left in him. But that's what the law requires. Who do I report to?' he asked me.

'I'm waiting for instructions,' I said. 'In the meantime, you'd better tell me and then put in a formal report in the morning.'

Dr Lasswade glanced round the room and then seemed to decide that the others knew so much already that if I did not mind them hearing what he had to say, then so be it. 'He's dead,' he said. 'I tell you that for what it's worth.'

'The body's been moved?' I asked.

'Of course it's been moved,' he said irritably. 'The

124

two constables fetched it out on to the bank for me. He was obviously dead, but how else could I confirm it? Did you think that I was going to put on frogman's gear and swim down to check his pulse?'

I had to agree, although I was sure that Superintendent McHarg would vent his temper on the subject at some later date. 'Could you make a preliminary guess as to when he died?' I asked.

'Not a hope. Some time between when he was last seen alive until . . . I was going to say until you found him, but he must have been dead for some hours. The ice was clinging to the body. Try the pathologist. If you can find out when the dead man ate his last meal, you may get some help.'

'Nor what he died of?'

'Now, there I may be able to help – subject, as always, to confirmation by the pathologist. You're sure . . . ?' His eyes indicated the other four occupants of the room.

'We've already seen him,' Deborah said. She shuddered. 'It was awful. Nothing you could say would be worse than that.' Mrs Brindle, who was looking subdued, nodded silently.

I was not leaving the warm room for the sake of confidentiality when the facts would no doubt be all over the district within a few hours. 'Go ahead,' I said.

'Very well. He was poisoned.' (I felt a sense of shock in the room.) 'I could be ninety-nine per cent certain that it was strychnine. The symptoms were typical. Opisthotonos.'

'He seemed to be bent over backwards,' Deborah said in a hushed voice.

'That's what I said. That and *risus sardonicus* – the grinning effect to which you took such exception,' he added to Mrs Brindle.

Hempie Wright put his face down in his hands. 'That's

what I saw through the ice,' he said. 'Him grinning up at me. Made me think of the way he'd look when his temper was going.'

'And that's all I can tell you,' the doctor said. 'Let's have a look at your face.'

Mrs Brindle refilled the teapot and then took herself off to bed. Somebody, she said, would have to be up and about in the morning – which was not very far away. Soon, we heard bathwater running.

The next few minutes were less than pleasant while the doctor washed the abraded side of my face and sterilised the scrapes, but when I caught sight of myself in a mirror my appearance, only slightly marred by a flesh-coloured plaster, would no longer have frightened horses.

During the doctor's ministrations, Allan Brindle took a phone-call. Now he hung up. 'That was the boss,' he said. 'Mr Jeffries himself in person. He seemed amused. In fact, he was laughing his head off. There's to be no prosecution over the poaching. He says there'll be no more. You hear that?' he asked Wright severely.

'I hear you.'

'Can I count on it?'

'Ask the laird.'

'I'll do that,' Brindle said and I thought that he probably would.

The doctor repacked his black bag. 'You should go home to bed,' he said. 'Take a day or two off work.' He was in the habit of giving the same advice for everything from ingrowing toenails to pregnancy, which is why his practice was booming.

'In the middle of a murder enquiry?' I said.

He shrugged.

The radio began to beep in the pocket of the coat which I had draped over the fireside irons. I dug it out.

'Superintendent McHarg's on his way,' said Control. 'He's at the top of Soutra now. Switch to Channel Eight and he can reach you.'

Wishing that I had left the radio in the snow, I switched to Channel Eight. Mr McHarg's voice came through immediately. He sounded as a superintendent of police might be expected to sound who had been fetched out of his bed in the small hours.

'Sergeant Fellowes?'

'Sir.'

'What the hell's going on? Can you speak freely?'

I glanced at Hempie Wright. Allan Brindle got to his feet. 'Come through into the kitchen,' he told Hempie. 'You can help me cut a few sandwiches.'

Deborah made herself small in her chair.

'I'm clear to speak now,' I said.

'Update me, from the end of your last report.'

It took nearly half an hour to give him all the details. When I finished with the doctor's tentative findings, he interrupted for the first time.

'Strychnine?' he said. 'That has to be premeditation. Where would somebody get strychnine in a hurry, in the middle of the night and out of the backwoods?'

Deborah looked up. 'Moles,' she said softly.

'Moles, sir,' I said, hoping to hell that she knew what she was talking about.

McHarg's voice became an incredulous squawk. 'Moles? You get strychnine from moles?'

'They use it to poison moles,' she whispered. 'Dip a worm in it and drop it into a mole-run.'

I passed the information on.

'Oh. That's the sort of work that man Wright does, isn't it?' he asked.

Deborah hesitated and then nodded. She was making warning faces.

127

'I believe so, sir,' I said. 'But he's not the only one.'

'You're thinking of the digger driver? I don't see him carrying strychnine around with him – unless you're going to tell me that they use it to clean diesel engines or some damn thing – and the Spanish police report that he's behaving just as you would expect a Brit on holiday to behave. Badly, that probably means. But there's no sign that he doesn't mean to return.'

Mrs Brindle had re-entered the room with a plate of sandwiches. She came and leaned over me. She was wearing a sensible dressing-gown hanging open over a very revealing nightdress. She smelled of bath salts and warm woman. She whispered into my ear, making a teasing gesture of it. 'Is that about Ron Campbell?' she asked. (I nodded.) 'Well, Allan and I went out for a drink after the shoot. Ron was in the bar and he was making a night of it with his mates. He was well on when I saw him, and no sign that he was planning an early night.'

She straightened up, pulled her dressing-gown around her and left the room. Deborah was looking at me sternly.

I had missed some of what McHarg had said. 'You have the man Wright there?' he was saying.

'In the next room.'

'Don't let go of him. It's clear what happened. Kerr shot a bird which flew on to the woods. He went to look for it and came across Wright, up to some of his tricks. Wright killed him. That's why he waited around until the other shooters had packed up. Then he carried him to the pond and pushed him under the ice. Eh?'

'The keeper says that Wright's boots were dry when he saw him later,' I pointed out. 'And you can't suddenly push strychnine into somebody's mouth in a fit of temper.'

'So somebody else was with him. That chap Youngson, the landowner. He'd have more to lose than Wright, if it were to come out that he was nothing but a bloody poacher. He'd be disgraced – and we could have jerked his gun permits. He went home early, but he could have come back – bringing Wright a flask of coffee or something, if they're as thick as you say,' Mr McHarg added in sudden inspiration. 'Kerr wouldn't hesitate to accept a hot drink from such a source while Youngson tried to convince him that there was an innocent explanation for whatever he'd seen. And Youngson lied to you about not knowing Wright's whereabouts.'

'That might have been because of the poaching,' I said.

'And it might not. Well?'

'There are still a number of anomalies to be explained,' I said.

'So explain them.'

'But—' I said. I stopped.

'You don't sound happy, Sergeant. But being happy isn't in your remit.'

'It sounds plausible,' I said, 'but I don't think it's what happened. More investigation . . .'

'What other explanation have you? Do you think you can make a case against Campbell?'

'No.'

He was still some miles off and yet I could see the expression which always came over his face when a subordinate was, in his view, being obstructive. 'I don't want somebody on this case who isn't wholeheartedly with me,' he said. 'We're making heavy going of it but I should be there in twenty minutes. The first thing we need is a positive identification. Go now, straight away, and break it to Mrs Kerr and ask her to come and identify the body. After that . . . we'll see about you and your hunches.'

The radio went dead.

'Is he always as nasty as that?' Deborah asked with her mouth full.

'Not always,' I said. I grabbed a sandwich. 'Usually. We'd better go. You're the chauffeur, so come and chauff. If you take me to my own car—'

'You'd get stuck without the jeep,' she said. 'And it's still not insured for you. I'm coming along.'

It was irregular but her reasoning was sound. My coat and boots were almost dry. We dressed and went out.

Dawn was close. The moon was still up but its light was paling in the new day. Beyond the jeep, a police Range Rover was waiting. A figure leaned out and beckoned. It was Mr Munro. I swallowed my sandwich and took one of the back seats. Deborah leaned into the jeep and started its engine.

'Mr McHarg wants me to set up an incident room,' Munro said. 'You know the geography. Would the big house be the place? Or is there an empty cottage?'

I answered the second question first. 'Not as far as I know. And if there is, it wouldn't have electricity and a telephone. The big house would be the place. Huge rooms, half of them not in use. But there's a snag. You'd need the laird's agreement.'

'I am aware that Superintendent McHarg has his suspicions about Mr Youngson. But Mr Youngson is not yet aware of that.'

'How—?' I bit off the question.

Chief Superintendent Munro could produce a very complacent smile on occasions and this was one of his best. 'Others can receive Channel Eight,' he said. 'What have you done with the man Wright?'

'He's inside in the care of the keeper.'

'We'll take him over until Mr McHarg arrives.' Mr Munro's proper function in the investigation would be solely to supply administrative and manpower support, but I could see that he intended to take more than a peripheral interest. 'I have been asked to provide every man who can be spared, for a search of the woods.'

It was not for me to comment. I held my peace.

Mr Munro nodded as though I had expressed my doubts. 'You agree then? A complete waste of time. All that he'll do is to obliterate the more recent tracks,' Mr Munro said cheerfully. 'And he called me an old fool!'

'He hasn't seen the ground yet,' I said, out of a dwindling sense of loyalty.

'And when he has, his pride will not allow him to admit that he was wrong. Off you go, then. See Mrs Kerr. Then report to me. I want to be sure that you're fit for duty. Your injury,' he added in explanation.

A few scratches down the side of the face could hardly be called an injury; but if a senior officer is being devious it does not pay to contradict.

When I got to the jeep, Deborah had vanished. She came out of Brindle's house again and hopped into the driving seat. 'I phoned Mum,' she said. 'When I didn't come in all night, she'd think . . . things.'

'And I know exactly what she'd think,' I said.

We were quiet, remembering what might have been and so nearly had been. Deborah drove carefully to the main road. 'What was that maneater whispering into your ear?' she asked suddenly. 'Not that you seemed to be enjoying the free peepshow,' she added in fairness.

'She and her husband went out for a drink after the pigeon-shoot. My favourite suspect was getting boozed up in the bar with a few friends.'

'Ron Campbell?'

'That's the one. It'll have to be checked with his friends, but it sounds as though he was too busy spending his holiday money to go back, put the injectors into the digger and bury Ian Kerr.'

'That leaves you back with Hempie Wright and Mr Youngson? I don't believe it. I can have hunches too.'

'It's too early for hunches,' I said. 'Mr McHarg was right about that.'

It was no more than two or three miles by road. Daylight was struggling to return. The fields were fresh and clean but already the road was furrowed by early travellers. We slowed to inch past a milk lorry. At Miscally Farm, lights were bright in the gloom of the day. Mrs Kerr seemed to fill the doorway as we got out of the jeep.

'You'd best come in,' she shouted.

We followed her into what had once been a traditional farmhouse kitchen but had now been modernised, equipped with the latest gadgetry and brightly decorated. At the plastic-topped table, a teenager was doing a jigsaw puzzle. He did not look up.

Mrs Kerr did not invite us to sit down. She faced me squarely, a stern, unbowed figure. 'Well?' she said. She opened her mouth again, ready to resume her demands for instant and miraculous results, but something in my face made her close it again.

'I'm sorry—' I began.

'Dear God!' Mrs Kerr said. She looked much older than her age. 'I can guess. But you'd better tell me.'

'A body has been found at McKimber. You'll have to go and make a formal identification.'

She looked a question at Deborah, who said, 'I've seen. I'm afraid there's no doubt.'

Mrs Kerr nodded, without asking how or when, and

began to remove her apron. I found that I had an admiration for her. The woman who had railed at me in my office was in command of herself, now that doubt was removed and her fears confirmed. 'I'll go right away,' she said. 'Can you bide and look after the laddie until I get back?'

'Of course,' Deborah said. 'But would you like me to come with you? It's not pretty.'

'Or would you like one of us to drive you?' I asked. 'The roads are tricky.'

'I could manage,' she said. 'But it's not worth starting a car. It's no distance over the fields. I'll take Ian's Land-Rover as far as the march and then walk. And I'm not one to take the vapours. I've seen some sights in my time.' She turned away to do something at the range. I thought that she surreptitiously wiped her eyes. 'If the laddie wants something to eat, let him have it. And help yourselves. I dare say you'll have been without breakfast?'

The rasp of a diesel engine and a rattle of loose metalwork sounded from the yard. I looked out. The ancient Land-Rover belonging to Keith's brother-in-law had arrived. Keith and Ronnie entered the house together.

'We just heard,' Keith said, avoiding my eye. 'We came to see if there was anything we could do.'

'It's all done for now,' Mrs Kerr said. 'We farming folk can't lie abed in the morning.'

'But later,' Deborah said. 'Will you be able to manage?'

Mrs Kerr's grim face softened. 'Bless you, we'll get by,' she said. 'My brother just has a smallholding but he's aye believed he'd make a grand farmer. Now's his chance to find out. And Ian – if it's him, which I'll no' be sure of until I've seen for myself – left us provided for.

133

When he and Brian took on the lease of a' that machinery, they took out insurances to pay off the bank loan if either of them . . . died.' Her voice nearly cracked on the word but she controlled it, indomitable. She took a tweed coat from behind the door and shrugged her bulk into it. 'Well, I'll just away and make it official,' she said briskly. 'Look after the laddie. I'll be quick as I can.'

'I think I should come with you,' Deborah said. 'It's not going to be easy.'

'No,' she said. 'It'll not be easy. I was hard on Ian. I'll be wishing . . . but it's too late for that now. Can't you see that I want to be alone?'

She stroked the boy's hair, roughly. He never looked up. Then she went out, closing the door gently behind her.

From the direction of the barn came the sound of a Land-Rover. It faded down through the fields. We waited until the noise had died away.

'Really, Dad!' Deborah said disgustedly. 'Pretending that you came over to help when it was nothing but sheer nosiness.'

'It was a bit of both,' Keith admitted cheerfully. 'We wanted to be sure that the widow-woman could manage on her own, though it seems that that one could manage very well even if her brother didn't come. But I also want to know what happened. I've had some thoughts.'

'I bet you have.'

'What thoughts?' I asked.

'Just thoughts,' Keith said. 'I won't know whether they could be the right ones unless you tell us what's been happening.'

'Nosiness!' Deborah said. 'Mrs Kerr told us to help ourselves. Did you have breakfast?'

'Hours ago,' Ronnie said. 'I could go another.'

'And I suppose I'm elected cook?' Deborah said.

'Best one for the job,' her father said.

'All right. How about you, young man? Hungry?'

The boy nodded without looking up from his jigsaw. He was not making good progress.

Farmhouse kitchens are never short of food. While Deborah fried eggs and bacon and some leftover sausages and Ronnie hacked away at a loaf, I recounted the events of the night. The meal was ready before I had finished.

'You've missed out one important detail,' Keith said when I had finished. 'How was he dressed?'

'I never saw him,' I said, 'except as a vague shape through the ice.'

Deborah was transferring food on to plates. 'I saw him,' she said. 'He'd lost his hat, if he'd had one. He was wearing a green Goretex coat, corduroys and Meindel boots. The coat was done up to his neck but it was open below and I saw a cartridge belt.'

'So he was still dressed for shooting,' Keith said. He filled his mouth and raised his eyebrows at me.

'That sounds like what he was wearing, the last time I saw him,' I said.

Keith nodded, chewed hastily and swallowed. 'He wouldn't have dressed like that to go off on a binge. On what he thought of as a social occasion, he was always smartly dressed. So it confirms that whatever happened to him happened on Saturday afternoon or evening.'

'But what?' I said. 'Everything I can think of has some serious flaw.'

'Shall we run over the possibilities?' Keith's words were disjointed as he alternated between eating and speech. 'Up to the time that it got dark and everybody swanned off, he certainly didn't head directly for here or he'd have passed us. If he walked off to the south or towards Nuttleigh's, you'd probably have seen him.'

'Definitely,' I said. 'I was facing south-west and watching the McKimber treetops, because that's where the birds were mostly coming from. If anything had moved lower down, the movement would have caught my peripheral vision.'

Keith emptied his mouth again. 'All right,' he said. 'That leaves McKimber, which is where he was found. Did he go there of his own accord? In pursuit of a shot bird, perhaps?'

'He knew there were shooters with dogs there,' Deborah said. 'If his bird flew on and dropped in the woods, somebody else would have picked it up before he got there. He'd have missed a dozen chances while they argued about it.'

'I'd've seen him,' Ronnie said. 'I was looking that way, between the wee wood and the McKimber March, and watching a tod – a fox, you ken? – as was skirting the edge of the woods. The wee dog gied me warning enough if birds was coming, and I was wondering would one of the Guns see the fox and give him both barrels before he got up his nerve and snatched yin of the shot birds.'

'What happened?' Deborah asked.

'That's not relevant,' Keith said. 'What did happen?' he asked Ronnie.

'A cushie dropped close to him and he made off wi't. I saw the Gun – that wee beggar Wright – hunting for his bird. I had to laugh. He was so sure the bird was there that he and his dog went round and around.'

'So much for that,' Keith said. 'Then we have the period between dusk and the time when you went back with Brian Dunbar.'

136

'Wright was definite,' I said. 'He stayed on. According to him, nobody moved in the direction of McKimber woods, nor parallel to them. If he didn't see them, he'd have heard them.'

'Which could be true,' Keith admitted. 'With only the faint glow of the clouds to shoot against, he'd have been listening as much as watching for the birds. On the other hand, if there's anything in McHarg's theory, Wright would lie his head off.'

'Nah,' Ronnie said.

Keith looked at him. 'You have a point to make?'

'Don't know about that,' Ronnie said bashfully. 'But I can't see Hempie Wright, nor Mr Youngson either, setting out to poison Ian Kerr to shut his mou'. They're not the criminal type. Just a pair of old gowks having a giggle at the keeper's expense. A clour wi' a rock if they'd lost the heid . . . well maybe.'

Keith had opened his mouth to say something when the boy spoke for the first time. He had a high, cracked voice but his words were clear. 'Dad's dead,' he said. He looked up. His expression was vacuous, but otherwise he looked like any other sturdy son of farming stock.

I can't speak for the other men but I know that I sat still, wondering what on earth to say. But Deborah got up quickly and put an arm round the boy's shoulders. 'I'm afraid so,' she said.

The boy moved suddenly and swept his jigsaw off the table. 'He never took me to the shooting,' he said. 'He was going to but he never did.'

'I'll come back some day and let you have a shot or two,' Keith said gently. (I tried to catch his eye. There had to be something in the Act which forbade the holder of a shotgun from lending it to somebody with a mental handicap, but for the moment I could not think of it.)

137

The boy smiled and then shook his head. 'What you were saying,' he said. There was a long pause while he thought about it. 'Dad never went to McKimber. After what Mr . . .' There was another long pause. 'After what Mister said to him, he said he'd never set foot on that land again.'

'Mr Brindle?' I suggested.

'Aye. He called Dad a word, but I can't tell you what it was because when I said it Mum said I was never to say it any more. After Mister said it to Dad, Dad said he'd never go on McKimber again.' He looked round anxiously to see whether he had made himself understood.

Deborah was down on her knees, collecting the pieces of the puzzle. 'But that's what people say when they're angry,' she said. 'They don't mean it.'

The boy sat silent again until I thought that his mind had wandered off again into some limbo of its own, but he was puzzling out the meaning of her words. 'Not Dad,' he said suddenly. 'He meant it. There was a lamb once,' he added as if that proved it.

'Lamb?' I said.

'Aye. Got through the fence. Dad wouldn't go after it. Sent me instead. Came all the way back to the house to fetch me. Dad never said anything he didn't mean. But he's dead now.' Deborah put the box with the pieces of puzzle back on the table and he went to work on it as though he had never seen it before.

After the long night without sleep, my mind was clogged with tiredness. 'But Mr Kerr was gone,' I said dully, 'before we went back down with Mr Dunbar.'

'You're absolutely sure?' Keith asked.

'We had Sam with us,' Deborah said. 'He was hunting for shot birds. Sam would soon have told us if a body had been hidden there.'

'You said that Brian Dunbar climbed up to the high seat. Nobody else?'

'No,' she said. 'But, Dad, the high seat's only a plank between two limbs of a big fir tree and a rail to lean back against. And I was shining a torch up into the branches in case there was a dead bird hung up. I'd have seen anything the size of a body.'

I glanced at the boy but he was intent on his puzzle. 'Dunbar couldn't have killed him,' I said. 'Mr Kerr was still shooting after Dunbar left. Or are you thinking that Brian Dunbar left a poisoned drink for him to take later on?'

'No,' Keith told me, 'I wasn't thinking any such thing. If that had happened, he couldn't have moved the body. You'd have found it in the hide when you went back. Let me put a couple of questions to you. I asked you, the following morning, how you'd dispatched any wounded birds and you said that you'd knocked their heads. You're sure that you didn't give one of them another shot on the ground, point blank?'

'Quite sure,' I said. Keith looked at me doubtfully.

'Of course he didn't,' Deborah said indignantly. 'I'd shown him how to do it properly and I'd have noticed if there'd been a bird or two in the bag which had been blown almost to bits.'

'I'll accept that,' Keith said. He looked at me again. 'There was a trailer beside where you were shooting the first time. Remember?'

'Of course I do,' I said. 'It was placed so that I was looking right into it.'

'When you went down there again with Brian Dunbar, did you notice anything different about it?'

I was about to deny it when my sluggish mind threw up the trace of a faint memory. 'There was something,' I said. 'I couldn't tell you what. And when I looked again in the morning, when you and I went back, it seemed to be the way I remembered it in daylight. It was only by moonlight and the glow of a torch that there was something different. I put it down to the different lighting.'

'There wasn't a body in it, if that's what you mean,' Deborah told Keith.

'It isn't.' He was still looking at me. 'Cast your mind back. What do you remember about the contents of the trailer?'

In the hypnotic stage of tiredness it was not difficult to conjure up the trailer. 'A large coil of fencing wire,' I said. 'Some sharpened fence-posts. A large hammer for driving them. A wooden box of small tools. Some rope. A large white polythene sack which seemed to be filled with similar sacks – from seed or fertiliser I suppose.'

'So far so good,' Keith said. 'Brian Dunbar uses his trailer the way a woman uses her handbag – it just fills up with all the things that might come in handy some day. Those things were there all three times you saw the trailer?'

I studied my mental picture again. 'I think so,' I said.

Keith was looking expectant. 'Wasn't there something else?' he said. 'Something that was missing when you saw it in darkness?'

'You saw it too,' I said. 'What have I forgotten?'

'I never looked inside it,' Keith said. 'I saw you look for fallen birds, so I didn't bother. But even if I had, it could be important that you remember without any prompting. Try again.'

I tried. I was about to give up when another little bit of the mental picture made a fuzzy appearance and then snapped into focus. 'A length of pipe,' I said. 'And something round. I didn't notice what. That's all I can remember and it's no good going on at me about it.'

140

'It's enough,' he said, leaning back in his chair. 'I'll be damned. The crazy idea that's been nagging at me turns out to be the truth after all. And Mrs Kerr handed us the motive on a plate.'

'You reckon?' Ronnie said. 'I thought you were havering when you spoke of it. But there was a whole lot of his barley uncut.'

'That's what was drawing the birds. We'd better get over to Nuttleigh's.'

This speaking in riddles was beginning to infuriate me. I was about to insist on an immediate explanation, but Mrs Kerr chose that moment to return, stamping the snow off her wellingtons. 'That's who it was, all right,' she said quietly. She gave the boy's ear a gentle pull. 'So you're the man of the house, at least 'til your uncle can get here. Go and make a start to feeding the beasts.'

The boy went out without a word.

Keith and Ronnie had slipped out but I hung on my heel for a moment. 'I'm sorry to pester you at such a time, but how many shotguns did Mr Kerr own?'

She looked at me dully. 'Just the one. The police have it now. It was in the pond with his body.'

'That's all right then.'

When I had the door open, she spoke once more in the softest voice I had ever heard her use. 'Wherever he is, do you think he kens that I'm sorry?'

'I'm sure he does,' I said. I almost ran to the jeep. The tears of such a huge woman would certainly be larger than life.

Those few words with Mrs Kerr, and a quick call on the radio to tell Control where I was going next, satisfied police routine but they also allowed Keith and Ronnie to pile into the Land-Rover and get well

141

ahead of us. Deborah set off after them. In my impatience I told her to get her skates on, but to my relief she ignored me and drove with care over the slippery surface.

'What the hell was that father of yours talking about?' I asked. Even to me, my voice sounded petulant.

'I don't know. Dad doesn't mean to tantalise,' she said in tones of apology. 'It's just that his mind goes shooting off ahead and he thinks that people are keeping up with him. Huh! I think that he thinks wrong – at least as far as I'm concerned.'

'Well,' I said, 'I think that you think that he thinks he knows how Ian Kerr was spirited away.'

'I do and I bet he does,' she said. We were twisting along the road between the two farm entrances. She slowed for the by-road to Nuttleigh's. 'What's more, I think I'm beginning to catch up with him. That piece of pipe in the trailer. Was it straight and about – oh – four feet long and sort of shaped? I mean, two different diameters?'

'That sounds about right,' I said. 'I didn't really notice the diameters. What was it?'

'And the round thing, was it blue or red?'

'Red,' I said as we pulled up in the farmyard. 'You're as bad as your father. Explain, for God's sake. I can't go into this, stone cold.'

The Land-Rover was parked beside the back door of the farmhouse. Ronnie was speaking to Mrs Dunbar at the door and Keith was beckoning to us urgently. They vanished inside, leaving the door ajar.

'I think we'd better go in,' Deborah said. 'But it's up to you. If we stop out here and have a debate about it, he won't wait for us – and he's quite capable of rushing ahead, conducting an interrogation, making accusations and even arresting somebody. Anyway, I could be wrong. It just doesn't seem to make sense. It's Dad's story. Let him bring it out.'

I made a last attempt to get the whole thing back on its proper course. 'If he knows all the answers, he must tell the police. Tell me, in fact. He mustn't go charging in—'

'Dad usually knows that he's doing.'

The word 'usually' was less than reassuring, but Deborah was already at the door. I bit back my protests and followed.

The back door led directly into the kitchen. To my eyes, coming direct from the kitchen at Miscally, it looked shabby. It lacked the latest gadgets, but its more old-fashioned utensils were arranged purposefully and to hand, I noticed, as though the room were a machine for the creation of meals rather than an entity existing for its own sake. Brian Dunbar, in his usual overalls, was washing greasy hands at the sink.

Mrs Dunbar, in a clean floral pinny, was fussing at the stove. 'This is nice,' she said. 'It's fine when folk just drop in. We're the same party as we were the night of the pigeon-shoot. You'll take tea? Or something stronger?' Her welcome was meant to be warm, but it was more reserved than it had been a few days earlier.

'We've just had breakfast,' I said. 'In fact, Keith and Ronnie have had two.'

'The tea's already in the pot.'

'Tea would be fine,' Keith said. Ronnie looked as though he would have preferred the 'something stronger'.

Brian dried his hands and went for more chairs. When we were seated, he said, 'What brings you over this way again so soon?' It seemed to me that the Dunbars both froze, waiting for the answer.

'We went to call on your neighbour,' Keith said.

143

'Mrs Kerr. Her husband's body was found in one of the ponds at McKimber. He seems to have died of poison.'

'He's been identified?' Brian asked.

'Yes. By his wife.'

'The poor woman,' Mrs Dunbar breathed. She sat down beside her husband and leaned against him. They had seemed to be a very close couple. Now I noticed that they seemed to be drawing comfort from tiny physical contacts.

There was silence in the room, so that I could hear a faint hum from the refrigerator.

Ronnie was the first to speak. He looked out of the window. 'It's not been a good year for you,' he said. He seemed to be fishing for comment rather than for a change of subject.

Brian Dunbar shook his head. 'Times are harder. It's not like it was a few years ago, with the grants and subsidies. Prices are well down.'

'It's just terrible,' Ronnie said. 'One bad year can break you. And you didn't get the most of your barley in before the big storm in September. That low ground of yours is badly drained.'

'That's true,' Brian said. 'I'm hoping that the water main track will improve the drainage.'

'You'll have it easier next year,' Keith said comfortingly. 'The insurance money will help.'

Mrs Dunbar looked at him sharply. 'Insurance?' she said.

'Yes. Tell me if I'm wrong. As I understand it,' Keith said, 'you and Ian Kerr equipped yourselves with a combine harvester, a drier and the latest in machinery by raising a joint bank loan. With interest rates shooting up, you must have had a sore trauchle keeping up with the payments. But you were each insured for enough to

144

pay off the debt if one of you died. The premiums would be another heavy outgoing which'll stop now.'

'That's quite true,' Brian said unhappily. 'But this is not the time to talk about such things.'

'The man's not long dead,' Mrs Dunbar said.

I had slipped down in my chair so that I could scribble surreptitiously on my knee. I thanked God that I had once taken the trouble to learn shorthand. The Dunbars were sitting close together on the other side of the table. From my low viewpoint, I could see that they had linked hands under the table and were gripping tightly.

In a high voice, Mrs Dunbar broke another silence. 'He must have taken his own life. God knows he had his troubles. But it's a mystery why he would do it at McKimber. I suppose he stayed late at the shooting and then walked over there.'

'There are witnesses who say not,' Keith said.

'Well, it's a sad business,' Brian said. 'And I suppose we'll have a new neighbour soon.'

'Likely her brother will come and run the place,' Mrs Dunbar said.

Keith ignored the attempt at a new subject. 'If that had been the way of it,' he said, 'it wouldn't explain why your Thunderbird was missing from the trailer when we went down in the dark and was back there again in the morning.'

In the silence which followed, Keith looked round our faces. Brian's face was scarlet but his wife's lips were white. When Keith's glance reached me, he realised that I had been left far behind. 'You must have seen and heard the bangers that farmers leave out to protect their crops?' he said. 'There are more sophisticated, electronic bird-scarers these days, but one of the simplest and cheapest is the Thunderbird. It's little

145

more than a long tube with a timer at one end which sparks a flint, at intervals that you can set between a minute or so up to perhaps a quarter of an hour. You couple it up to a gas cylinder. There's a small reservoir which mixes gas and air together. When the mixture fires, it sounds pretty much like a gunshot.

'It's my guess that Ian Kerr left the wee wood in the back of Brian's Land-Rover.'

'But that couldn't be,' Brian said hoarsely. He looked at me. 'You know that he was still shooting after I left him. You could see for yourself.'

'That's true,' Deborah said.

'Not quite,' Keith told her. 'You heard a shot and Brian called your attention to it. What you saw was a few feathers hanging in the air. It would look just as it looks when a pigeon has been killed overhead. But you'd get the same effect if somebody had hauled the Thunderbird up to the high seat, stuffed a handful of feathers into the mouth of it and set the timer for a long delay. That would be when he noticed your lofted decoys, of course, and realised that he'd have to bring them back to you. Otherwise, you'd have gone back for them and found Ian Kerr and the Thunderbird.'

Deborah looked as though she were being torn between doubt and enlightenment. 'But, Dad,' she said unhappily, 'that's not possible. As the light faded, everybody would see the flash high in the treetops.'

'Not if he knew that the gas cylinder was almost empty,' Keith said, 'or, more likely, if he opened the valve and let nearly all of the gas escape. As the gas runs out, those things start misfiring some of the times the timer sparks, because the mixture's too weak, until they soon stop firing altogether.'

Deborah was still unconvinced. 'But . . . but . . . I suppose the plank may have been wide enough that I

146

wouldn't see the scarer when I shone the torch up there. Not if it was lying flat along the plank. But, Dad, a red gas cylinder? I couldn't have missed that.'

My mind was getting its second wind and I suddenly saw an answer that Deborah had missed. 'The first time Mr Dunbar came down, he brought the food in a green carrier bag,' I said. 'When he came again, he was carrying the thermos flask in his hand and the sausage rolls in the paper bag. Among the evergreen branches, by torchlight, would you have noticed a carefully placed, green carrier bag?'

Deborah thought about it, her smooth brow furrowed. 'No,' she said at last. 'I don't believe I would.'

'You came back during the night, of course,' Keith said to Brian Dunbar. 'You returned the scarer and the cylinder to the trailer. And you also took Ian Kerr's body round by road and pushed it under the ice. He had to be found, for the sake of the insurance, but not on your land or his own. Somewhere else, and later, when the motivation and the sequence of events would be less obvious. A delay would – literally – muddy the evidence.'

The Dunbars had been sitting quietly, looking from Deborah to her father and back again as if they were spectators at a tennis match, awaiting an outcome in which they were interested but not concerned. Now Brian Dunbar stirred in his chair. 'It's a good story,' he said shakily. 'It has a ring to it. But where's your evidence?'

'Under the snow,' Keith said. 'Feathers.'

I began to see a little more daylight. 'Is this why you kept asking me how I'd killed any wounded birds?' I asked him.

Keith seemed surprised that I should have to ask the question. 'Of course. I noticed that one or two of the feathers which were lying around showed signs of scorching. If you hadn't been giving wounded birds the *coup de grâce* with a shot at point blank range, then how else, I wondered, could feathers have been exposed to flame? Those feathers will still be there,' he added. 'Come the thaw, they can be found again. And I don't suppose Brian thought it necessary to replace the gas cylinder with a full one.'

'That seems to be that, then,' Brian Dunbar said slowly.

His wife twisted round to look into his face. 'Brian, are you sure?'

He nodded. 'Let's not prolong the agony. It's over.'

I remembered that I was a policeman. 'I must warn you,' I said, 'that anything you say—'

'I know all that,' Dunbar said impatiently. 'It was just as Keith said. After I'd killed him—'

'Brian, no!' his wife said.

'I know what I'm doing, Chrissie. It's best that we get it over. I knew that there were other men, up on McKimber ground, but mostly they were back among the trees. Even if they weren't, I could get the stuff out of the trailer and the body into the Land-Rover without being seen, they were parked so close to the fence. I let all but the last wee puff of gas out of the cylinder. The risk I had to take was that one of the men would see the feathers come out of the treetops, or know that there wasn't a bird there when the banger fired.'

'You had a busy night after that,' Keith said.

'Aye, what with getting the stuff down from the high seat and then moving the body round to McKimber.' He looked at me. 'What happens now?'

I was about to say that I was taking him into custody when his wife spoke up. 'What he's been telling you is

148

just moonshine,' she said. 'He knew nothing until Ian Kerr was dead.'

Brian took her by the arms and shook her tenderly. 'Chrissie!' he wailed. 'Hold your wheesht. It's better my way.'

'It's not,' she said bravely. 'And I can't let you. Brian knew nothing. It wasn't for the sake of the money, not directly. That never entered my head,' she told me and it seemed important to her that I believed her. 'I knew how sick to his heart Brian was, watching all that we'd worked for going down the drain. And Ian could have spared us that if he'd cared to bend a wee bit. Last year it was his turn to have first call on the machinery. Back at harvest time, when the forecast was of heavy rain to come and the charts were showing great swirls of black cloud coming in from the Atlantic, he'd got the best of his barley in. His soil's sandier than ours, it drains in a day, but ours is clay and those lower fields can go like a pond. When the rain's heavy, water drains off McKimber and we're flooded.' She paused and heaved a long sigh. 'It was good barley, it'd have gone for malting.'

'You don't know that,' Brian said.

'Aye, I do. It wouldn't have cost Ian more than pennies to let us have the use of the combine. We could have got most of it in before the rain arrived. But he insisted that we stuck to the letter of our agreement. I went and begged him, but it was no use. Then we tried to hire from outside, but a'body else was in the same boat. So we lost the best part of our year's income and we still had to pay up for the insurance and the bank loan.

'Brian was so miserable he was hardly sleeping a wink. I was worried for him. Even so, we might have ridden it out.' A furious scowl took command of her usually placid face. 'But then Ian had the chowk to come and shoot here, because the birds were coming in to our

149

barley – which was still spoiling in the ground because
he was too thrawn to help a neighbour. That made me
mad. Not just angry, I mean, but really mad. I must
have been out of my mind.' She pulled her hand out
of her husband's grasp in order to hide her face. Her
voice continued, muffled, from between her fingers. 'I
was making up the flasks and food to send down to our
guests – because that's how I thought of you, as guests,
all except Ian. And it came over me why should I feed
him?' She looked up and laced her fingers again with
Brian's. 'And yet I couldn't not. You see, he was a
visitor,' she explained shyly.

'I understand,' Keith said.

'I think you do. I took the wee bottle of stuff that
Brian used for the moles and I tipped it into one of the
flasks and I told Brian that that one was for Ian and to
make sure that nobody else drank it, because that was
the way Ian liked his coffee. I was sorry, after.'

'Chrissie, Chrissie,' Brian said. 'It was better my
way. They'll have me anyway as an accessory.'

'There, pet.' I saw her give his hand a squeeze.
'They'll go easier on you than if you'd done the whole
of it.' She looked at Keith rather than at me. Keith was
the one who would understand. 'When Ian drank the
coffee and died, Brian guessed at once what I'd done.
He decided right then how to cover it up. He can be
very quick,' she said proudly.

'It was an awfu' way for a man to go,' Brian said.
'That's terrible stuff. But she wouldn't know that,' he
added quickly. 'I nearly picked up his gun to put him
out of it. But then he just . . . went.'

'If I'd known how it would be,' she said, 'I'd have
thought again. As it was, I was sorry after Brian had
gone and I ran after him.'

'That's so,' Brian said. 'I met her running down the

track as I was coming back here. Too late, of course, by far. But at least she tried.'

'You don't need to fret any more, love,' Chrissie Dunbar said. 'The worst of it's over, the not knowing. It won't be so bad. And I couldn't have borne to have you put away and to have to carry on with folk talking behind my back. We'll just have to live it out. We'll be together again, in time, and there should be some money left after the farm's sold up. No' a lot, but we'll have the pension soon after. We'll get by.'

They were both looking at me as the symbol of the law. 'If you've made up your minds,' I said, 'would you care to write out statements in your own hands and your own words? Start by saying that you're making them of your free will and without threats or inducements and then just tell it as it happened.'

'I don't think that you should,' Keith said. Now that the riddle was solved, he had turned his coat. 'Not until you've seen a solicitor. I could fetch Mr Enterkin.'

They shook their heads in unison. 'We'll not make a last-ditch battle of it,' Brian said.

'We did a bad thing between us,' Chrissie Dunbar added. 'Now we'll pay for it. The sooner we get it all over the better.'

'If you say so,' Keith said. 'Would you like us to see to the beasts? We could arrange for them to be looked after until they and the standing crops and machinery can be sold.'

'That'd be a weight off our minds,' Brian agreed. 'We're grateful.' He held out his hand and Keith and Ronnie both shook it firmly. They kissed Chrissie Dunbar on the cheek before making their escape. Such farewells seemed hard to understand until I realised that forgiveness was being exchanged.

Brian got out paper and found two pens and soon

151

they were writing away, almost happily, pausing to confirm times with each other or to ask the spelling of a word.

We were quiet in the room, quiet enough to hear the sound of a vehicle which approached quietly and stopped fifty yards short of the house. I got up and went outside.

Chief Superintendent Munro was approaching the house on foot, walking softly. 'I was told that you were here,' he said. 'There had to be a reason.'

'There is,' I said. 'Mrs Dunbar killed Ian Kerr and Mr Dunbar transported the body. They're writing out their confessions now.'

Mr Munro managed not to smile, but I could see the enjoyment flooding through him. 'Very interesting,' he said. He lowered his voice. 'Superintendent McHarg is busy at this very moment, harassing Hempie Wright and Mr Youngson. We'll give him a little more rope. Once I hear over the radio that he's brought them in, then we'll move. And I think he'll find that the laird has a great deal more clout around Edinburgh than he supposes. Mr Youngson knows the Scottish Secretary, and I've seen him with my own eyes going off for dinner with the Chief Constable. You can leave this to me, Sergeant. It's best that you go off and have your face seen to.'

'Is that an order?' I asked.

'It is. I'll confirm it with Mr McHarg. Come in and make a full report in the morning.'

We went inside. Dunbar looked up and saw the uniformed figure. 'We're almost done,' he said. 'If you give us a minute to attend to things, we'll be ready to come with you.'

'Take your time,' Mr Munro said. 'There's no hurry. Just no hurry at all.'

Chrissie Dunbar pushed aside the papers and got up.

152

'If we're not leaving just yet,' she said, 'I'll put something on for the lunch.'

We sat in the jeep, wondering what to do now that the excitement was over.

'I feel sad, all of a sudden,' Deborah said.

A policeman, dealing every day with human tragedies, has to learn not to become emotionally involved, but I knew what she meant. 'Don't be,' I said. 'Mrs Kerr has a broad back. She'll be all right.'

'It's not just for the Kerrs. The Dunbars were such a nice couple. She was pushed too far and she over-reacted. Now they'll be apart for a long time, and that's the one thing they'll find hard to bear.'

'The way the law works these days, it may not be so very long.' A quick change of subject seemed to be needed before we became maudlin. 'While Mr Munro coaxes Superintendent McHarg out on to a limb prior to sawing it off,' I said, 'I think I'd better be out of the way.'

'Shall we go back to your flat? I seem to remember that our conversation was interrupted, last night.'

'We will,' I said, 'but that's for later.' Evening and soft lights would be needed if we were to re-establish the mood. Besides, I had another idea. 'Let's go out to the club and shoot a round of Sporting.'

'It's cold and I'm tired,' Deborah said. 'I don't think I'll be a damn bit of good.' She smiled suddenly. 'Come on, then. Let's do it.'